The two of them had been journeying across the interminable parched wastes of the Outback for many days now—how many, not even the Elder Gods could tell. They were ambassadors, these two: Their Excellencies Robert E. Howard and H.P. Lovecraft of the Kingdom of New Holy Diabolic England, envoys of His Britannic Majesty Henry VIII to the court of Prester John.

In another life they had been writers, fantasists, inventors of fables; but now they found themselves caught up in something far more fantastic than anything to be found in any of their tales, for this was no fable, this was no fantasy. This was the reality of Hell.

"Robert—" said the pale man nervously.

"A lot like Texas, yes," Howard went on, "only Hell's just a faint carbon copy of the genuine item. Just a rough first draft, is all. You see that sandstorm rising out thataway? We had sandstorms, they covered entire counties! You see that lightning? In Texas that would be just a flicker!"

"If you could drive just a little more slowly, Bob—"

"More slowly? Cthulhu's whiskers, man, I am driving slowly!"

"Yes, I'm quite sure you believe that you are."

"And the way I always heard it, H.P., you loved for people to drive you around at top speed. Seventy, eighty miles an hour, that was what you liked best, so the story goes."

—from GILGAMESH IN THE OUTBACK

SCIENCE FICTION GRAND MASTERS SERIES

The Award Winning and Nominated Stories of

ROBERT SILVERBERG

DANGEROUS DIMENSIONS
Includes the Hugo Award Winning Story, *NIGHTWINGS*

AROUND THE CONTINUUM
Includes the Hugo Award Winning Story, *GILGAMESH IN THE OUTBACK*

BEYOND THE BEYOND
Including the Nebula Award Winning Story, *PASSENGERS*

ACROSS THE EONS
Includes the Nebula Award Winning Story, *SAILING TO BYZANTIUM*

WONDERS AND MARVELS
Includes the Hugo Award Winning Story, *ENTER A SOLDIER. LATER: ENTER ANOTHER*

GALACTIC TRAVELERS
Includes the Nebula Award Winning Story, *GOOD NEWS FROM THE VATICAN*

FUTURES UNLIMITED
Includes the Nebula Award Winning Story, *BORN WITH THE DEAD*

www.WonderPublishingGroup.com
www.WonderEbooks.com

AROUND THE CONTINUUM

ROBERT SILVERBERG

WONDER PUBLISHING GROUP

Published by
Wonder Publishing Group Books,
a division of Wonder Audiobooks LLC Northville, MI 48167

ISBN: 978-1-61013-094-3

ACKNOWLEDGMENTS

"Gilgamesh in the Outback" ©1987 by Agberg, Ltd. Originally published in ASIMOV'S SCIENCE FICTION, July, 1986.
"Sundance," ©1969, 1987 by Agberg, Ltd. Originally published in FANTASY AND SCIENCE FICTION, July, 1969.
"In Entropy's Jaws," ©1971 by Agberg, Ltd. Originally published in INFINITY 2.
"Schwartz Between the Galaxies," ©1974 by Agberg, Ltd.Originally published in STELLAR 1.
"Gianni," ©1982 by Agberg, Ltd. Originally published in PLAYBOY, February, 1982.

Cover art by Alex Martinez

www.WonderPublishingGroup.com
www.WonderEbooks.com

CONTENTS

INTRODUCTION

The five stories collected here amassed ten awards nominations and one win. "Gilgamesh in the Outback" was nominated for the Nebula, Hugo, Locus, SF Chronicle, and Asimov's Readers' Poll awards, and won the Hugo. "Sundance" was a Nebula nominee, though I withdrew it from the final ballot so that it would not compete with another story of mine (which won the award.) "Schwartz Between the Galaxies" was a Hugo nominee and also was nominated for the Locus award. "In Entropy's Jaws" and "Gianni" both were Locus award nominees.

The oldest of these stories is "Sundance," which I wrote in 1968 for FANTASY AND SCIENCE FICTION when it was under the editorship of Edward L. Ferman. "In Entropy's Jaws" dates from 1971, and was written for the anthology INFINITY 2, edited by Bob Hoskins. "Schwartz Between the Galaxies," a 1974 story, was done for Judy-Lynn Del Rey, the editor of the anthology STELLAR 1.

"Gianni," from 1981, was the first of my many contributions to PLAYBOY, whose fiction editor then was Alice Turner. It appeared in the February, 1982 issue. "Gilgamesh in the Outback", written in 1986, was commissioned by Janet Morris, the editor of the shared-world anthology REBELS IN HELL, but it was published first in the July, 1986 issue ASIMOV'S SCIENCE FICTION, Gardner Dozois, editor. A few years later I incorporated it into my novel, TO THE LAND OF THE LIVING, in a somewhat revised form.

—Robert Silverberg

GILGAMESH IN THE OUTBACK

Faust. First I will question thee about hell.
Tell me, where is the place that men call hell?
Meph. Under the heavens.
Faust. Ay, but whereabout?
Meph. Within the bowels of these elements,
Where we are tortur'd and remain for ever:
Hell hath no limits, nor is circumscrib'd
In one self place; for where we are is hell,
And where hell is, there must we ever be:
And, to conclude, when all the world dissolves,
And every creature shall be purified,
All places shall be hell that are not heaven.
Faust. Come, I think hell's a fable.
Meph. Ay, think so still, till experience change thy mind.

Marlowe: *Dr. Faustus*

* * * *

Jagged green lightning danced on the horizon and the wind came ripping like a blade out of the east, skinning the flat land bare and sending up clouds of gray-brown dust.

Gilgamesh grinned broadly. By Enlil, now that was a wind! A lion-killing wind it was, a wind that turned the air dry and crackling. The beasts of the field gave you the greatest joy in their hunting when the wind was like that, hard and sharp and cruel.

He narrowed his eyes and stared into the distance, searching for this day's prey. His bow of several fine woods, the bow that no man but he was strong enough to draw—no man but he and Enkidu his beloved thrice-lost friend—hung loosely from his hand. His body was poised and ready. Come now, you beasts! Come and be slain! It is Gilgamesh, king of Uruk, who would make his sport with you this day!

Other men in this land, when they went about their hunting, made use of guns, those foul machines that the New Dead had brought, which hurled death from a great distance along with much noise and fire and smoke; or they employed the even deadlier laser devices from whose ugly snouts came spurts of blue-white flame. Cowardly things, all those killing machines! Gilgamesh loathed them, as he did most instruments of the New Dead, those slick and bustling Johnny-come-latelies of Hell. He would not touch them if he could help it. In all the thousands of years he had dwelled in this nether world he had never used any weapons but those he had known during his first lifetime: the javelin, the spear, the double-headed axe, the hunting bow, the good bronze sword. It took some skill, hunting with such weapons as those. And there was physical effort; there was more than a little risk. Hunting was a contest, was it not? Then it must make demands. Why, if the idea was merely to slaughter one's prey in the fastest and easiest and safest way, then the sensible thing to do would be to ride high above the hunting grounds in a weapons platform and drop a little nuke, eh, and lay waste five kingdoms' worth of beasts at a single stroke!

He knew that there were those who thought him a fool for such ideas. Caesar, for one. Cocksure cold-blooded Julius with the gleaming pistols thrust into his belt and the submachine gun slung across his shoulders. "Why don't you admit it?" Caesar had asked him once, riding up in his jeep as Gilgamesh was making ready to set forth toward Hell's open wilderness. "It's a pure affectation, Gilgamesh, all this insistence on arrows and javelins and spears. This isn't old Sumer you're living in now."

Gilgamesh spat. "Hunt with 9-millimeter automatics? Hunt with grenades and cluster bombs and lasers? You call that sport, Caesar?"

"I call it acceptance of reality. Is it technology you hate? What's the difference between using a bow and arrow and using a gun? They're both technology, Gilgamesh. It isn't as though you kill the animals with your bare hands."

"I have done that, too," said Gilgamesh.

"Bah! I'm on to your game. Big hulking Gilgamesh, the simple innocent oversized Bronze Age hero! That's just an affectation, too, my friend! You pretend to be a stupid, stubborn thick-skulled barbarian because it suits you to be left alone to your hunting and your wandering, and that's all you claim that you really want. But secretly you regard yourself as superior to anybody who lived in an era softer than your own. You mean to restore the bad old filthy ways of the ancient ancients, isn't that so? If I read you the right way you're just biding your time, skulking around with your bow and arrow in the dreary Outback until you think it's the right moment to launch the putsch that carries you to supreme power here. Isn't that it, Gilgamesh? You've got some crazy fantasy of overthrowing Satan himself and lording it over all of us. And then we'll live in mud cities again and make little chicken scratches on clay tablets, the way we were meant to do. What do you say?"

"I say this is great nonsense, Caesar."

"Is it? This place is full of kings and emperors and sultans and pharaohs and shahs and presidents and dictators, and every single one of them wants to be Number One again. My guess is that you're no exception."

"In this you are very wrong."

"I doubt that. I suspect you believe you're the best of us all; you, the sturdy warrior, the great hunter, the maker of bricks, the builder of vast temples and lofty walls, the shining beacon of ancient heroism. You think we're all decadent rascally degenerates and that you're the one true virtuous man. But you're as proud and ambitious as any of us. Isn't that how it is? You're a fraud, Gilgamesh, a huge musclebound fraud!"

"At least I am no slippery tricky serpent like you, Caesar, who dons a wig and spies on women at their mysteries if it pleases him."

Caesar looked untroubled by the thrust. "And so you pass three-quarters of your time killing stupid monstrous creatures in the Outback and you make sure everyone knows that you're too pious to have anything to do with modern weapons while you do it. You don't fool me. It isn't virtue that keeps you from doing your killing with a decent double-barreled .470 Springfield. It's intellectual pride, or maybe simple laziness. The bow just happens to be the weapon you grew up with, who knows how many thousands of years ago. You like it because it's familiar. But what language are you speaking now, eh? Is it your thick-tongued Euphrates gibberish? No, it seems to be English, doesn't it? Did you grow up speaking English too, Gilgamesh? Did you grow up riding around in jeeps and choppers? Apparently some of the new ways are acceptable to you."

Gilgamesh shrugged. "I speak English with you because that is what is spoken now in this place. In my heart I speak the old tongue, Caesar. In my heart I am still Gilgamesh of Uruk, and I will hunt as I hunt."

"Uruk's long gone to dust. This is the life after life, my friend. We've been here a long time. We'll be here for all time to come, unless I miss my guess. New people constantly bring new ideas to this place, and it's impossible to ignore them. Even you can't do it. Isn't that a wristwatch I see on your arm, Gilgamesh? A digital watch, no less?"

"I will hunt as I hunt," said Gilgamesh. "There is no sport in it, when you do it with guns. There is no grace in it."

Caesar shook his head. "I never could understand hunting for sport, anyway. Killing a few stags, yes, or a boar or two, when you've bivouacked in some dismal Gaulish forest and your men want meat. But hunting? Slaughtering hideous animals that aren't even edible? By Apollo, it's all nonsense to me!"

"My point exactly."

"But if you must hunt, to scorn the use of a decent hunting rifle—"

"You will never convince me."

"No," Caesar said with a sigh. "I suppose I won't. I should know better than to argue with a reactionary."

"Reactionary! In my time I was thought to be a radical," said Gilgamesh. "When I was king in Uruk—"

"Just so," Caesar said, laughing. "King in Uruk. Was there ever a king who wasn't reactionary? You put a crown on your head and it addles your brains instantly. Three times Antonius offered me a crown, Gilgamesh. Three times, and—"

"—you did thrice refuse it, yes. I know all that. 'Was this ambition?' You thought you'd have the power without the emblem. Who were you fooling, Caesar? Not Brutus, so I hear. Brutus said you were ambitious. And Brutus—"

That stung him. "Damn you, don't say it!"

"—was an honorable man," Gilgamesh concluded, enjoying Caesar's discomfiture.

Caesar groaned. "If I hear that line once more—"

"Some say this is a place of torment," said Gilgamesh serenely. "If in truth it is, yours is to be swallowed up in another man's poetry. Leave me to my bows and arrows, Caesar, and return to your jeep and your trivial intrigues. I am a fool and a reactionary, yes. But you know nothing of hunting. Nor do you understand anything of me."

* * * *

All that had been a year ago, or two, or maybe five—with or without a wristwatch, there was no keeping proper track of time in Hell, where the unmoving ruddy eye of the sun never budged from the sky—and now Gilgamesh was far from Caesar and all his minions, far from the troublesome center of Hell and the tiresome squabbling of those like Caesar and Alexander and Napoleon and that sordid little Guevara man who maneuvered for power in this place.

Let them maneuver all they liked, those shoddy new men of the latter days. Some day they might learn wisdom, and was not that the purpose of this place, if it had any purpose at all?

Gilgamesh preferred to withdraw. Unlike the rest of those fallen emperors and kings and pharaohs and shahs, he felt no yearning to reshape Hell in his own image. Caesar was as wrong about Gilgamesh's ambitions as he was about the reasons for his preferences in hunting gear. Out here in the Outback, in the bleak dry chilly hinterlands of Hell, Gilgamesh hoped to find peace. That was all he wanted now: peace. He had wanted much more, once, but that had been long ago.

There was a stirring in the scraggly underbrush.

A lion, maybe?

No, Gilgamesh thought. There were no lions to be found in Hell, only the strange nether-world beasts. Ugly hairy things with flat noses and many legs and dull baleful eyes, and slick shiny things with the faces of women and the bodies of malformed dogs, and worse, much worse. Some had drooping leathery wings, and some were armed with spiked tails that rose like a scorpion's, and some had mouths that opened wide enough to swallow an elephant at a gulp. They all were demons of one sort or another, Gilgamesh knew. No matter. Hunting was hunting; the prey was the prey; all beasts were one in the contest of the field. That fop Caesar could never begin to comprehend that.

Drawing an arrow from his quiver, Gilgamesh laid it lightly across his bow and waited.

* * * *

"If you ever had come to Texas, H.P., this here's a lot like what you'd have seen," said the big barrel-chested man with the powerful arms and the deeply tanned skin. Gesturing sweepingly with one hand, he held the wheel of the Land Rover lightly with three fingers of the other, casually guiding the vehicle in jouncing zigs and zags over the flat trackless landscape. Gnarled gray-green shrubs matted the gritty ground. The sky was black with swirling dust. Far off in the distance barren mountains rose like dark jagged teeth. “Beautiful. Beautiful. As close to Texas in look as makes no never mind, this countryside is.”

“Beautiful?” said the other man uncertainly. “Hell?”

“This stretch sure is. But if you think Hell’s beautiful, you should have seen Texas!”

The burly man laughed and gunned the engine, and the Land Rover went leaping and bouncing onward at a stupefying speed.

His traveling companion, a gaunt, lantern-jawed man as pale as the other was bronzed, sat very still in the passenger seat, knees together and elbows digging in against his ribs, as if he expected a fiery crash at any moment. The two of them had been journeying across the interminable parched wastes of the Outback for many days now—how many, not even the Elder Gods could tell. They were ambassadors, these two: Their Excellencies Robert E. Howard and H.P. Lovecraft of the Kingdom of New Holy Diabolic England, envoys of His Britannic Majesty Henry VIII to the court of Prester John.

In another life they had been writers, fantasists, inventors of fables; but now they found themselves caught up in something far more fantastic than anything to be found in any of their tales, for this was no fable, this was no fantasy. This was the reality of Hell.

"Robert—" said the pale man nervously.

"A lot like Texas, yes," Howard went on, "only Hell's just a faint carbon copy of the genuine item. Just a rough first draft, is all. You see that sandstorm rising out thataway? We had sandstorms, they covered entire counties! You see that lightning? In Texas that would be just a flicker!"

"If you could drive just a little more slowly, Bob—"

"More slowly? Cthulhu's whiskers, man, I am driving slowly!"

"Yes, I'm quite sure you believe that you are."

"And the way I always heard it, H.P., you loved for people to drive you around at top speed. Seventy, eighty miles an hour, that was what you liked best, so the story goes."

"In the other life one dies only once, and then all pain ceases," Lovecraft replied. "But here, where one can go to the Undertaker again and again, and when one returns one remembers every final agony in the brightest of hues—here, dear friend Bob, death's much more to be feared, for the pain of it stays with one forever, and one may die a thousand deaths." Lovecraft managed a pale baleful smile. "Speak of that to some professional warrior, Bob, some Trojan or Hun or Assyrian—or one of the gladiators, maybe, someone who has died and died and died again. Ask him about it: the dying and the rebirth, and the pain, the hideous torment, reliving every detail. It is a dreadful thing to die in Hell. I fear dying here far more than I ever did in life. I will take no needless risks here."

Howard snorted. "Gawd, try and figure you out! When you thought you lived only once, you made people go roaring along with you on the highway a mile a minute. Here where no one stays dead for very long you want me to drive like an old woman. Well, I'll attempt it, H.P., but everything in me cries out to go like the wind. When you live in big country, you learn to cover the territory the way it has to be covered. And Texas is the biggest country there is. It isn't just a place, it's a state of mind."

"As is Hell," said Lovecraft. "Though I grant you that Hell isn't Texas."

"Texas!" Howard boomed. "God damn, I wish you could have seen it! By god, H.P., what a time we'd have had, you and me, if you'd come to Texas. Two gentlemen of letters like us riding together all to hell and gone from Corpus Christi to El Paso and back again, seeing it all and telling each other wondrous stories all the way! I swear, it would have enlarged your soul, H.P. Beauty such as perhaps even you couldn't have imagined. That big sky. That blazing sun. And the open space! Whole empires could fit into Texas and never be seen again! That Rhode Island of yours, H.P.—we could drop it down just back of Cross Plains and lose it behind a medium-size prickly pear! What you see here, it just gives you the merest idea of that glorious beauty. Though I admit this is plenty beautiful itself, this here."

"I wish I could share your joy in this landscape, Robert," Lovecraft said quietly, when it seemed that Howard had said all he meant to say.

"You don't care for it?" Howard asked, sounding surprised and a little wounded.

"I can say one good thing for it: at least it's far from the sea."

"You'll give it that much, will you?"

"You know how I hate the sea and all that the sea contains! Its odious creatures—that hideous reek of salt air hovering above it—" Lovecraft shuddered fastidiously. "But this land—this bitter desert—you don't find it somber? You don't find it forbidding?"

"It's the most beautiful place I've seen since I came to Hell."

"Perhaps the beauty is too subtle for my eye. Perhaps it escapes me altogether. I was always a man for cities, myself."

"What you're trying to say, I reckon, is that all this looks real hateful to you. Is that it? As grim and ghastly as the Plateau of Leng, eh, H.P.?" Howard laughed. " 'Sterile hills of gray granite...dim wastes of rock and ice and snow....' " Hearing himself quoted, Lovecraft laughed too, though not exuberantly. Howard went on. "I look around at the Outback of Hell and I see something a whole lot like Texas, and I love it. For you it's as sinister as dark frosty Leng, where people have horns and hooves and munch on corpses and sing hymns to Nyarlathotep. Oh, H.P., H.P., there's no accounting for tastes, is there? Why, there's even some people who—whoa, now! Look there!"

He braked the Land Rover suddenly and brought it to a jolting halt. A small malevolent-looking something with blazing eyes and a scaly body had broken from cover and gone scuttering across the path just in front of them. Now it faced them, glaring up out of the road, snarling and hissing flame.

"Hell-cat!" Howard cried. "Hell-coyote! Look at that critter, H.P. You ever see so much ugliness packed into such a small package? Scare the toenails off a shoggoth, that one would!"

"Can you drive past it?" Lovecraft asked, looking dismayed.

"I want a closer look, first." Howard rummaged down by his boots and pulled a pistol from the clutter on the floor of the car. "Don't it give you the shivers, driving around in a land full of critters that could have come right out of one of your stories, or mine? I want to look this little ghoul-cat right in the eye."

"Robert—"

"You wait here. I'll only be but a minute."

Howard swung himself down from the Land Rover and marched stolidly toward the hissing little beast, which stood its ground. Lovecraft watched fretfully. At any moment the creature might leap upon Bob Howard and rip out his throat with a swipe of its horrid yellow talons, perhaps—or burrow snout-deep into his chest, seeking the Texan's warm, throbbing heart—

They stood staring at each other, Howard and the small monster, no more than a dozen feet apart. For a long moment neither one moved. Howard, gun in hand, leaned forward to inspect the beast as one might look at a feral cat guarding the mouth of an alleyway. Did he mean to shoot it? No, Lovecraft thought: beneath his bluster the robust Howard seemed surprisingly squeamish about bloodshed and violence of any sort.

Then things began happening very quickly. Out of a thicket to the left a much larger animal abruptly emerged: a ravening Hell-creature with a crocodile head and powerful thick-thighed legs that ended in monstrous curving claws. An arrow ran through the quivering dewlaps of its heavy throat from side to side, and a hideous dark ichor streamed from the wound down the beast's repellent blue-gray fur. The small animal, seeing the larger one wounded this way, instantly sprang upon its back and sank its fangs joyously into its shoulder. But a moment later there burst from the same thicket a man of astonishing size, a great dark-haired black-bearded man clad only in a bit of cloth about his waist. Plainly he was the huntsman who had wounded the larger monster, for there was a bow of awesome dimensions in his hand and a quiver of arrows on his back. In utter fearlessness the giant plucked the foul little creature from the wounded beast's back and hurled it far out of sight; then, swinging around, he drew a gleaming bronze dagger, and with a single fierce thrust, drove it into the breast of his prey as the coup de grace that brought the animal crashing heavily down.

All this took only an instant. Lovecraft, peering through the window of the Land Rover, was dazzled by the strength and speed of the dispatch and awed by the size and agility of the half-naked huntsman. He glanced toward Howard, who stood to one side, his own considerable frame utterly dwarfed by the black-bearded man.

For a moment Howard seemed dumbstruck, paralyzed with wonder and amazement. But then he was the first to speak.

"By Crom," he muttered, staring at the giant. "Surely this is Conan of Aquilonia and none other!" He was trembling. He took a lurching step toward the huge man, holding out both his hands in a strange gesture—submission, was it? "Lord Conan?" Howard murmured. "Great king, is it you? Conan? Conan?" And before Lovecraft's astounded eyes Howard fell to his knees next to the dying beast, and looked up with awe and something like rapture in his eyes at the towering huntsman.

* * * *

It had been a decent day's hunting so far. Three beasts brought down after long and satisfying chase; every shaft fairly placed; each animal skillfully dressed, the meat set out as bait for other hell-beasts, the hide and head carefully put aside for proper cleaning at nightfall. There was true pleasure in work done so well.

Yet there was a hollowness at the heart of it all, Gilgamesh thought, that left him leaden and cheerless no matter how cleanly his arrows sped to their mark. He never felt that true fulfillment, that clean sense of completion, that joy of accomplishment, which was ultimately the only thing he sought.

Why was that? Was it—as the Christian dead so drearily insisted—because this was Hell, where by definition there could be no delight?

To Gilgamesh that was foolishness. Those who came here expecting eternal punishment did indeed get eternal punishment, and it was even more horrendous than anything they had anticipated. It served them right, those true believers, those gullible New Dead, that army of credulous Christians.

He had been amazed when their kind first came flocking into Hell, Enki only knew how many thousands of years ago. The things they talked of! Rivers of boiling oil! Lakes of pitch! Demons with pitchforks! That was what they expected, and the Administration was happy to oblige them. There were Torture Towns aplenty for those who wanted them. Gilgamesh had trouble understanding why anyone would. Nobody among the Old Dead really could figure them out, those absurd New Dead with their obsession with punishment. What was it Sargon called them? Masochists, that was the word. Pathetic masochists. But then that sly little Machiavelli had begged to disagree, saying, "No, my lord, it would be a violation of the nature of Hell to send a true masochist off to the torments. The only ones who go are the strong ones—the bullies, the braggarts, the ones who are cowards at the core of their souls." Augustus had had something to say on the matter too, and Caesar, and that Egyptian bitch Hatshepsut had butted in, she of the false beard and the startling eyes, and then all of them had jabbered at once, trying yet again to make sense of the Christian New Dead. Until finally Gilgamesh had said, before stalking out of the room, "The trouble with all of you is that you keep trying to make sense out of this place. But when you've been here as long as I have—"

Well, perhaps Hell *was* a place of punishment. Certainly there were some disagreeable aspects to it. The business about sex, for example. Never being able to come, even if you pumped away all day and all night. And the whole digestive complication, allowing you to eat real food but giving you an unholy hard time when it came to passing the stuff through your gut. But Gilgamesh tended to believe that those were merely the incidental consequences of being dead: this place was not, after all, the land of the living, and there was no reason why things should work the same way here as they did back there.

He had to admit that the reality of Hell had turned out to be nothing at all like what the priests had promised it would be. The House of Dust and Darkness, was what they had called it in Uruk long ago. A place where the dead lived in eternal night and sadness, clad like birds, with wings for garments. Where the dwellers had dust for their bread, and clay for their meat. Where the kings of the earth, the masters, the high rulers, lived humbly without their crowns, and were forced to wait on the demons like servants. Small wonder that he had dreaded death as he had, believing that that was what awaited him for all time to come!

Well, in fact all that had been mere myth and folly. Gilgamesh could still remember Hell as it had been when he first had come to it: a place much like Uruk, so it seemed, with low flat-roofed buildings of whitewashed brick, and temples rising on high platforms of many steps. And there he found all the heroes of olden days, living as they had always lived: Lugalbanda, his father, and Enmerkar, his father's father; and Ziusudra who built the vessel by which mankind survived the Flood; and others on and on, back to the dawn of time. At least that was what it was like where Gilgamesh first found himself; there were other districts, he discovered later, that were quite different—places where people lived in caves, or in pits in the ground, or in flimsy houses of reeds, and still other places where the Hairy Men dwelled and had no houses at all. Most of that was gone now, greatly transformed by all those who had come to Hell in the latter days, and indeed a lot of nonsensical ugliness and ideological foolishness had entered in recent centuries in the baggage of the New Dead. But still, the idea that this whole vast realm—infinitely bigger than his own beloved Land of the Two Rivers—existed merely for the sake of chastising the dead for their sins, struck Gilgamesh as too silly for serious contemplation.

Why, then, was the joy of his hunting so pale and hollow? Why none of the old ecstasy when spying the prey, when drawing the great bow, when sending the arrow true to its mark?

Gilgamesh thought he knew why, and it had nothing to do with punishment. There had been joy aplenty in the hunting for many a thousand years of his life in Hell. If the joy had gone from it now, it was only that in these latter days he hunted alone; that Enkidu—his friend, his true brother, his other self—was not with him. That and nothing but that: for he had never felt complete without Enkidu since they first had met and wrestled and come to love one another after the manner of brothers, long ago in the city of Uruk. That great burly man, broad and tall and strong as Gilgamesh himself, that shaggy wild creature out of the high ridges: Gilgamesh had never loved anyone as he loved Enkidu.

But it was the fate of Gilgamesh, so it seemed, to lose him again and again. Enkidu had been ripped from him the first time long ago when they still dwelled in Uruk, on that dark day when the gods had had revenge upon them for their great pride and had sent the fever to take Enkidu's life. In time Gilgamesh too had yielded to death and was taken into

Hell, which he found nothing at all like the Hell that the scribes and priests of the Land had taught; and there he had searched for Enkidu, and one glorious day he had found him. Hell had been a much smaller place, then, and everyone seemed to know everyone else; but even so it had taken an age to track him down. Oh, the rejoicing that day in Hell! Oh, the singing and the dancing, the vast festival that went on and on! There was great kindliness among the denizens of Hell in those days, and everyone was glad for Gilgamesh and Enkidu. Minos of Crete gave the first great party in honor of their reunion, and then it was Amenhotep's turn, and then Agamemnon's. And on the fourth day the host was dark slender Varuna, the Meluhhan king, and then on the fifth the heroes gathered in the ancient hall of the Ice-Hunter folk where one-eyed Vy-otin was chieftain and the floor was strewn with mammoth tusks, and after that—

Well, and it went on for some long time, the great celebration of the reunion. This was long before the hordes of New Dead had come, all those grubby little unheroic people out of unheroic times, carrying with them their nasty little demons and their dark twisted apparatus of damnation and punishment. Before they had come, Hell had simply been a place to live in the time after life. It was all very different then, a far happier place.

For uncountable years Gilgamesh and Enkidu dwelled together in Gilgamesh's palace in Hell as they had in the old days in the Land of the Two Rivers. And all was well with them, with much hunting and feasting, and they were happy in Hell even after the New Dead began to come in, bringing all their terrible changes.

They were shoddy folk, these New Dead, confused of soul and flimsy of intellect, and their petty trifling rivalries and vain strutting poses were a great nuisance. But Gilgamesh and Enkidu kept their distance from them while they replayed all the follies of their lives, their nonsensical Crusades and their idiotic trade wars and their preposterous theological squabbles. The trouble was that they had brought not only their lunatic ideas to Hell but also their accursed diabolical modern gadgets, and the worst of those were the vile weapons called guns, that slaughtered noisily from afar in the most shameful cowardly way. Heroes know how to parry the blow of a battle-ax or the thrust of a sword; but what can even a hero do about a bullet from afar? It was Enkidu's bad luck to fall between two quarreling bands of these gun-wielders, a flock of babbling Spaniards and a rabble of arrogant Englanders, for whom he tried to make peace. Of course they would have no peace, and soon shots were flying, and Gilgamesh arrived at the scene just as a bolt from an arquebus tore through his dear Enkidu's noble heart.

No one dies in Hell forever; but some are dead a long time, and that was how it was with Enkidu. It pleased the Undertaker this time to keep him in limbo some hundreds of years, or however many it was—tallying such matters in Hell is always difficult. It was, at any rate, a dreadful long while, and Gilgamesh once more felt that terrible inrush of loneliness that only the presence of Enkidu might cure. Hell continued to change, and now the changes were coming at a stupefying, overwhelming rate. There seemed to be far more people in the world than there ever had been in the old days, and great armies of them marched into Hell every day, a swarming rabble of uncouth strangers who after only a little interval of disorganization and bewilderment would swiftly set out to reshape the whole place into something as discordant and repellent as the world they had left behind. The steam engine came, with its clamor and clangor, and something called the dynamo, and then harsh glittering electrical lights blazed in every street where the lamps had been, and factories arose and began pouring out all manner of strange things. And more and more and more, relentlessly, unceasingly. Railroads. Telephones. Automobiles. Noise, smoke, soot everywhere, and no way to hide from it. The Industrial Revolution, they called it. Satan and his swarm of Administration bureaucrats seemed to love all the new things, and so did almost everyone else, except for Gilgamesh and a few other cranky conservatives. "What are they trying to do?" Rabelais asked one day. "Turn the place into Hell?" Now the New Dead were bringing in such devices as radios and helicopters and computers, and everyone was speaking English, so that once again Gilgamesh, who had grudgingly learned the new-fangled Greek long ago when

Agamemnon and his crew had insisted on it, was forced to master yet another tongue-twisting, intricate language. It was a dreary time for him. And then at last did Enkidu reappear, far away in one of the cold northern domains. He made his way south, and for a time, they were reunited again, and once more all was well for Gilgamesh of Uruk in Hell.

But now they were separated again, this time by something colder and more cruel than death itself. It was beyond all belief, but they had quarreled. There had been words between them, ugly words on both sides—such a dispute as never in thousands of years had passed between them in the land of the living or in the land of Hell—and at last Enkidu had said that which Gilgamesh had never dreamed he would ever hear, which was, "I want no more of you, king of Uruk. If you cross my path again I will have your life." Could that have been Enkidu speaking, or was it, Gilgamesh wondered, some demon of Hell in Enkidu's form?

In any case he was gone. He vanished into the turmoil and intricacy of Hell and placed himself beyond Gilgamesh's finding. And when Gilgamesh sent forth inquiries, back came only the report, "He will not speak with you. He has no love for you, Gilgamesh."

It could not be. It must be a spell of witchcraft, thought Gilgamesh. Surely this was some dark working of the Hell of the New Dead, that could turn brother against brother and lead Enkidu to persist in his wrath. In time, Gilgamesh was sure, Enkidu would be triumphant over this sorcery that gripped his soul, and he would open himself once more to the love of Gilgamesh. But time went on, after the strange circuitous fashion of Hell, and Enkidu did not return to his brother's arms.

What was there to do but hunt, and wait, and hope?

* * * *

So this day Gilgamesh hunted in Hell's parched Outback. He had killed and killed and killed again, and now late in the day he had put his arrow through the throat of a monster more foul even than the usual run of creatures of Hell; but there was a terrible vitality to the thing, and it went thundering off, dripping dark blood from its pierced maw.

Gilgamesh gave pursuit. It is sinful to strike and wound and not to kill. For a long weary hour he ran, crisscrossing this harsh land. Thorny plants slashed at him with the malevolence of imps, and the hard wind flailed him with clouds of dust sharp as whips. Still the evil-looking beast outpaced him, though its blood drained in torrents from it to the dry ground.

Gilgamesh would not let himself tire, for there was god-power in him by virtue of his descent from the divine Lugalbanda, his great father who was both king and god. But he was hard pressed to keep going. Three times he lost sight of his quarry, and tracked it only by the spoor of its blood-droppings. The bleak red motionless eye that was the sun of

Hell seemed to mock him, hovering forever before him as though willing him to run without cease.

Then he saw the creature, still strong but plainly staggering, lurching about at the edge of a thicket of little twisted, greasy-leaved trees. Unhesitatingly Gilgamesh plunged forward. The trees stroked him lasciviously, coating him with their slime, trying like raucous courtesans to insinuate their leaves between his legs; but he slapped them away, and emerged finally into a clearing where he could confront his animal.

Some repellent little hell-beast was clinging to the back of his prey, ripping out bloody gobbets of flesh and ruining the hide. A Land Rover was parked nearby, and a pale, strange-looking man with a long jaw was peering from its window. A second man, red-faced and beefy-looking, stood close by Gilgamesh's roaring, snorting quarry.

First things first. Gilgamesh reached out, scooped the foul hissing little carrion-seeker from the bigger animal's back, flung it aside. Then with all his force he rammed his dagger toward what he hoped was the heart of the wounded animal. In the moment of his thrust Gilgamesh felt a great convulsion within the monster's breast and its hell-life left it in an instant.

The work was done. Again, no exultation, no sense of fulfillment; only a kind of dull ashen release from an unfinished chore. Gilgamesh caught his breath and looked around.

What was this? The red-faced man seemed to be having a crazy fit. Quivering, shaking, sweating, dropping to his knees, his eyes gleaming insanely—

"Lord Conan?" the man cried. "Great king?"

"Conan is not one of my titles," said Gilgamesh, mystified. "And I was a king once in Uruk, but I reign over nothing at all in this place. Come, man, get off your knees!"

"But you are Conan to the life!" moaned the red-faced man hoarsely. "To the absolute life!"

Gilgamesh felt a surge of intense dislike for this fellow. He would be slobbering in another moment. Conan? Conan? That name meant nothing at all. No, wait; he had known a Conan once, some little Celtic fellow he had encountered in a tavern, a chap with a blunt nose and heavy cheekbones and dark hair tumbling down his face, a drunken twitchy little man forever invoking forgotten godlets of no consequence—yes, he had called himself Conan, so Gilgamesh thought. Drank too much, caused trouble for the barmaid, even took a swing at her, that was the one. Gilgamesh had dropped him down an open cesspool to teach him manners. But how could this blustery-faced fellow here mistake me for that one? He was still mumbling on, too, babbling about lands whose names meant nothing to Gilgamesh—Cimmeria, Aquilonia, Hyrkania, Zamora. Total nonsense. There were no such places.

And that glow in the fellow's eyes—what sort of look was that? A look of adoration, almost the sort of look a woman might give a man when she has decided to yield herself utterly to his will.

Gilgamesh had seen such looks aplenty in his day, from women and men both; and he had welcomed them from women, but never from a man. He scowled. What does he think I am? Does he think, as so many have wrongly thought, that because I loved Enkidu with so great a love that I am a man who will embrace a man in the fashion of men and women? Because it is not so. Not even here in Hell is it so, said Gilgamesh to himself. Nor will it ever be.

"Tell me everything!" the red-faced man was imploring. "All those exploits that I dreamed in your name, Conan: Tell me how they really were! That time in the snow fields, when you met the frost giant's daughter—and when you sailed the *Tigress* with the Black Coast's queen—and that time you stormed the Aquilonian capital, and slew King Numedides on his own throne—"

Gilgamesh stared in distaste at the man groveling at his feet.

"Come, fellow, stop this blather now," he said sourly. "Up with you! You mistake me greatly, I think."

The second man was out of the Land Rover now, and on his way over to join them. An odd-looking creature he was, too, skeleton-thin and corpse-white, with a neck like a water-bird's that seemed barely able to support his long, big-chinned head. He was dressed oddly too, all in black, and swathed in layer upon layer as if he dreaded the faintest chill.

Yet he had a gentle and thoughtful way about him, quite unlike the wild-eyed and feverish manner of his friend. He might be a scribe, Gilgamesh thought, or a priest; but what the other one could be, the gods alone would know.

The thin man touched the other's shoulder and said, "Take command of yourself, man. This is surely not your Conan here."

"To the life! To the very life! His size—his grandeur—the way he killed that beast—"

"Bob—Bob, Conan's a figment! Conan's a fantasy! You spun him out of whole cloth. Come, now. Up. Up." To Gilgamesh he said, "A thousand pardons, good sir. My friend is—sometimes excitable—"

Gilgamesh turned away, shrugging, and looked to his quarry. He had no need for dealings with these two. Skinning the huge beast properly might take him the rest of the day; and then to haul the great hide back to his camp, and determine what he wanted of it as a trophy—

Behind him he heard the booming voice of the red-faced man. "A figment, H.P.? How can you be sure of that? I thought I invented Conan, too; but what if he really lived, what if I had merely tapped into some powerful primordial archetype, what if the authentic Conan stands here before us this very moment—"

"Dear Bob, your Conan had blue eyes, did he not? And this man's eyes are dark as night."

"Well—" Grudgingly.

"You were so excited you failed to notice. But I did. This is some barbarian warrior, yes, some great huntsman beyond any doubt—a Nimrod, an Ajax. But not Conan, Bob! Grant him his own identity. He's no invention of yours." Coming up beside Gilgamesh, the long-jawed man said, speaking in a formal and courtly way, "Good sir, I am Howard Phillips Lovecraft, formerly of Providence, Rhode Island, and my companion is Robert E. Howard of Texas, whose other life was lived, as was mine, in the twentieth century after Christ. At that time we were tale-tellers by trade, and I think he confuses you with a hero of his own devising. Put his mind at ease, I pray you, and let us know your name."

Gilgamesh looked up. He rubbed his wrist across his forehead to clear it of a smear of the monster's gore and met the other man's gaze evenly. This one, at least, was no madman, strange though he looked.

Quietly Gilgamesh said, "I think his mind may be beyond putting at any ease. But know you that I am called Gilgamesh, the son of Lugalbanda."

"Gilgamesh the Sumerian?" Lovecraft whispered. "Gilgamesh who sought to live forever?"

"Gilgamesh am I, yes, who was king in Uruk when that was the greatest city of the Land of the Two Rivers, and who in his folly thought there was a way of cheating death."

"Do you hear that, Bob?"

"Incredible. Beyond all belief!" muttered the other.

Rising until he towered above them both, Gilgamesh drew in his breath deeply and said with awesome resonance, "I am Gilgamesh to whom all things were made known, the secret things, the truths of life and death, most especially those of death. I have coupled with Inanna the goddess in the bed of the Sacred Marriage; I have slain demons and spoken with gods; I am two parts god myself, and only one part mortal." He paused and stared at them, letting it sink in, those words that he had recited so many times in situations much like this. Then in a quieter tone he went on, "When death took me I came to this nether world they call Hell, and here I pass my time as a huntsman, and I ask you now to excuse me, for as you see I have my tasks."

Once more he turned away.

"Gilgamesh!" said Lovecraft again in wonder. And the other said, "If I live here till the end of time, H.P., I'll never grow used to it. This is more fantastic than running into Conan would have been! Imagine it: *Gilgamesh!*"

A tiresome business, Gilgamesh thought: all this awe, all this adulation.

The problem was that damned epic, of course. He could see why Caesar grew so irritable when people tried to suck up to him with quotations out of Shakespeare's verses. "Why, man, he doth bestride the narrow world like a Colossus," and all that: Caesar grew livid by the third syllable. Once they put you into poetry, Gilgamesh had discovered, as had Odysseus and Achilles and Caesar after him and many another, your own real self can begin to disappear and the self of the poem overwhelms you entirely and turns you into a walking cliché. Shakespeare had been particularly villainous that way, Gilgamesh thought: ask Richard III, ask Macbeth, ask Owen Glendower. You found them skulking around Hell with perpetual chips on their shoulders, because every time they opened their mouths people expected them to say something like "My kingdom for a horse!" or "Is this a dagger which I see before me?" or "I can call spirits from the vasty deep." Gilgamesh had had to live with that kind of thing almost from the time he had first come to Hell, for they had written the poems about him soon after. All that pompous brooding stuff, a whole raft of Gilgamesh tales of varying degrees of basis in reality. And then the Babylonians and the Assyrians, and even those smelly garlic-gobbling Hittites, had gone on translating and embroidering them for another thousand years so that everybody from one end of the known world to the other knew them by heart. And even after all those peoples were gone and their languages had been forgotten, there was no surcease, because these twentieth-century folk had found the whole thing and deciphered the text somehow and made it famous all over again. Over the centuries they had turned him into everybody's favorite all-purpose hero, which was a hell of a burden to bear: there was a piece of him in the Prometheus legend, and in the Heracles stuff, and in that story of Odysseus' wanderings, and even in the Celtic myths, which was probably why this creepy Howard fellow kept calling him Conan. At least that other Conan, that ratty little sniveling drunken one, had been a Celt. Enlil's ears, but it was wearying to have everyone expecting you to live up to the mythic exploits of twenty or thirty very different culture-heroes! And embarrassing, too, considering that the original non-mythical Heracles and Odysseus and some of the others dwelled here too and tended to be pretty possessive about the myths that had attached to them, even when they were simply variants on his own much older ones.

There was substance to the Gilgamesh stories, of course, especially the parts about him and Enkidu. But the poet had salted the story with a lot of pretentious arty nonsense too, as poets always will, and in any case you got very tired of having everybody boil your long and complex life down into the same twelve chapters and the same little turns of phrase. It got so that Gilgamesh found himself quoting the main Gilgamesh poem too, the one about his quest for eternal life—well, that one wasn't too far from the essence of the truth, though they had mucked up a lot of the details with precious little "imaginative" touches—by way of making introduction for himself: "I am the man to whom all things were made known, the secret things, the truths of life and death." Straight out of the poet's mouth, those lines. Tiresome. Tiresome. Angrily he jabbed his dagger beneath the dead monster's hide, and set about his task of flaying, while the two little men behind him went on muttering and mumbling to one another in astonishment at having run into Gilgamesh of Uruk in this bleak and lonely corner of Hell.

* * * *

There were strange emotions stirring in Robert Howard's soul, and he did not care for them at all. He could forgive himself for believing for that one giddy moment that this Gilgamesh was his Conan. That was nothing more than the artistic temperament at work, sweeping him up in a bit of rash feverish enthusiasm. To come suddenly upon a great muscular giant of a man in a loincloth who was hacking away at some fiendish monster with a little bronze dagger, and to think that he must surely be the mighty Cimmerian—well, that was a pardonable enough thing. Here in Hell you learned very quickly that you might run into anybody at all. You could find yourself playing at dice with Lord Byron or sharing a mug of mulled wine with Menelaos or arguing with Plato about the ideas of Nietzsche, who was standing right there making faces, and after a time you came to take most such things for granted, more or less.

So why not think that this fellow was Conan? No matter that Conan's eyes had been of a different color. That was a trifle. He looked like Conan in all the important ways. He was of Conan's size and strength. And he was kingly in more than physique. He seemed to have Conan's cool intelligence and complexity of soul, his regal courage and indomitable spirit.

The trouble was that Conan, the wondrous Cimmerian warrior from 19,000 B.C., had never existed except in Howard's own imagination. And there were no fictional characters in Hell. You might meet Richard Wagner, but you weren't likely to encounter Siegfried. Theseus was here somewhere, but not the Minotaur. William the Conqueror, yes; William Tell, no.

That was all right, Howard told himself. His little fantasy of meeting Conan here in Hell was nothing but a bit of mawkish narcissism: he was better off without it. Coming across the authentic Gilgamesh—ah, how much more interesting that was! A genuine Sumerian king—an actual titan out of history's dawn, not some trumped-up figure fashioned from cardboard and hard-breathing wish-fulfilling dreams. A flesh-and-blood mortal who lived a lusty life and had fought great battles and had walked eye to eye with the ancient gods. A man who had struggled against the inevitability of death, and who in dying had taken on the immortality of mythic archetype—ah, now there was someone worth getting to know! Whereas Howard had to admit that he would learn no more from a conversation with Conan than he could discover by interrogating his own image in the mirror. Or else a meeting with the "real" Conan, if it was in any way possible, would surely cast him into terrible confusions and contradictions of soul from which there would be no recovering. No, Howard thought. Better that this man be Gilgamesh than Conan, by all means. He was reconciled to that.

But this other business—this sudden bewildering urge to throw himself at the giant's feet, to be swept up in his arms, to be crushed in a fierce embrace—

What was that? Where had *that* come from? By the blazing Heart of Ahriman, what could it mean?

Howard remembered a time in his former life when he had gone down to the Cisco Dam and watched the construction men strip and dive in: well-built men, confident, graceful, at ease in their bodies. For a short while he had looked at them and had reveled in their physical perfection. They could have been naked Greek statues come alive, a band of lusty Apollos and Zeuses. And then as he listened to them shouting and laughing and crying out in their foul-mouthed way he began to grow angry, suddenly seeing them as mere thoughtless animals who were the natural enemies of dreamers like himself. He hated them as the weak always must hate the strong, those splendid swine who could trample the dreamers and their dreams as they wished. But then he had reminded himself that he was no weakling himself, that he who once had been spindly and frail had by hard effort made himself big and strong and burly. Not beautiful of body as these men were—too fleshy for that, too husky—but nevertheless, he had told himself, there was no man there whose ribs he could not crush if it came to a struggle. And he had gone away from that place full of rage and thoughts of bloody violence.

What had that been all about? That barely suppressed fury—was it some sort of dark hidden lust, some craving for the most bestial sort of sinfulness? Was the anger that had arisen in him masking an anger he should have directed at himself, for looking upon those naked men and taking pleasure in it?

No. No. No. No. He wasn't any kind of degenerate. He was certain of that.

The desire of men for men was a mark of decadence, of the decline of civilization. He was a man of the frontier, not some feeble limp-wristed sodomite who reveled in filth and wanton evil. If he had never in his short life known a woman's love, it was for lack of opportunity, not out of a preference for that other shameful kind. Living out his days in that small and remote prairie town, devoting himself to his mother and to his writing, he had chosen not to avail himself of prostitutes or shallow women, but he was sure that if he had lived a few years longer and the woman who was his true mate had ever made herself known to him, he would certainly have reached toward her in passion and high abandon.

And yet—and yet—that moment when he first spied the giant Gilgamesh, and thought he was Conan—

That surge of electricity through his entire body, and most intensely through his loins—what else could it have been but desire, instant and intense and overwhelming? For a man? Unthinkable! Even this glorious hero—even this magnificent kingly creature—

No. No. No. No.

I am in Hell, and this is my torment, Howard told himself.

He paced furiously up and down alongside the Land Rover. Desperately he fought off the black anguish that threatened to settle over him now, as it had done so many times in his former life and in this life after life. These sudden corrupt and depraved feelings, Howard thought: they are nothing but diabolical perversions of my natural spirit, intended to cast me into despair and self-loathing! By Crom, I will resist! By the breasts of Ishtar, I will not yield this foulness!

All the same he found his eyes straying to the edge of the nearby thicket, where Gilgamesh still knelt over the animal he had killed.

What extraordinary muscles rippling in that broad back, in those iron-hard thighs! What careless abandon in the way he was peeling back the creature's shaggy hide, though he had to wallow in dark gore to do it! That cascade of lustrous black hair lightly bound by a jewelled circlet, that dense black beard curling in tight ringlets—

Howard's throat went dry. Something at the base of his belly was tightening into a terrible knot.

Lovecraft said, "You want a chance to talk with him, don't you?"

Howard swung around. He felt his cheeks go scarlet. He was utterly certain that his guilt must be emblazoned incontrovertibly on his face.

"What the hell do you mean?" he growled. His hands knotted of their own accord into fists. There seemed to be a band of fire across his forehead. "What would I want to talk with him about, anyway?"

Lovecraft looked startled by the ferocity of Howard's tone and posture. He took a step backward and threw up his hand almost as though to protect himself. "What a strange thing to say! You, of all people, with your love of antique times, your deep and abiding passion for the lost mysteries of those steamy Oriental empires that perished so long ago! Why, man, is there nothing you want to know about the kingdoms of Sumer? Uruk, Nippur, Ur of the Chaldees? The secret rites of the goddess Inanna in the dark passageways beneath the ziggurat? The incantations that opened the gates of the Underworld, the libations that loosed and bound the demons of the worlds beyond the stars? Who knows what he could tell us? There stands a man six thousand years old, a hero from the dawn of time, Bob!"

Howard snorted. "I don't reckon that oversized son of a bitch would want to tell us a damned thing. All that interests him is getting the hide off that bloody critter of his."

"He's nearly done with that. Why not wait, Bob? And invite him to sit with us a little while. And draw him out, lure him into telling us tales of life beside the Euphrates!" Now Lovecraft's dark eyes were gleaming as though he too felt some strange lust, and his forehead was surprisingly bright with uncharacteristic perspiration; but Howard knew that in Lovecraft's case what had taken possession of him was only the lust for knowledge, the hunger for the arcane lore of high antiquity that Lovecraft imagined would spill from the lips of this Mesopotamian hero. That same lust ached in him as well. To speak with this man who had lived before Babylon was, who had walked the streets of Ur when Abraham was yet unborn—

But there were other lusts besides that hunger for knowledge, sinister lusts that must be denied at any cost—

"No," said Howard brusquely. "Let's get the hell out of here right now, H.P. This damned foul bleak countryside is getting on my nerves."

Lovecraft gave him a strange look. "But weren't you just telling me how beautiful—"

"Damnation take whatever I was telling you! King Henry's expecting us to negotiate an alliance for him. We aren't going to get the job done out here in the boondocks."

"The what?"

"Boondocks. Wild uncivilized country. Term that came into use after our time, H.P. The backwoods, you know? You never did pay much heed to the vernacular, did you?" He tugged at Lovecraft's sleeve. "Come on. That big bloody ape over there isn't going to tell us a thing about his life and times, I guarantee. Probably doesn't remember anything worth telling, anyway. And he bores me. Pardon me, H.P., but I find him an enormous pain in the butt, all right? I don't have any further hankering for his company. Do you mind, H.P.? Can we move along, do you think?"

"I must confess that you mystify me sometimes, Bob. But of course if you—" Suddenly Lovecraft's eyes widened in amazement. "Get down, Bob! Behind the car! Fast!"

"What—"

An arrow came singing through the air and passed just alongside Howard's left ear. Then another, and another. One arrow ricocheted off the flank of the Land Rover with a sickening thunking sound. Another struck straight on and stuck quivering an inch deep in the metal.

Howard whirled. He saw horsemen—a dozen, perhaps a dozen and a half—bearing down on them out of the darkness to the east, loosing shafts as they came.

They were lean compact men of some Oriental stock in crimson leather jerkins, riding like fiends. Their mounts were little flat-headed, fiery-eyed gray Hell-horses that moved as if their short, fiercely pistoning legs could carry them to the far boundaries of the nether world without the need of a moment's rest.

Chanting, howling, the yellow-skinned warriors seemed to be in a frenzy of rage. Mongols? Turks? Whoever they were, they were pounding toward the Land Rover like the emissaries of Death himself. Some brandished long wickedly curved blades, but most wielded curious-looking small bows from which they showered one arrow after another with phenomenal rapidity.

Crouching behind the Land Rover with Lovecraft beside him, Howard gaped at the attackers in a paralysis of astonishment. How often had he written of scenes like this? Waving plumes, bristling lances, a whistling cloud of cloth-yard shafts! Thundering hooves, wild war cries, the thunk of barbarian arrowheads against Aquilonian shields! Horses rearing and throwing their riders.... Knights in bloodied armor tumbling to the ground.... Steel-clad forms littering the slopes of the battlefield....

But this was no swashbuckling tale of Hyborean derring-do that was unfolding now. Those were real horsemen—as real as anything was, in this place—rampaging across this chilly wind-swept plain in the outer reaches of Hell. Those were real arrows; and they would rip their way into his flesh with real impact and inflict real agony of the most frightful kind.

He looked across the way at Gilgamesh. The giant Sumerian was hunkered down behind the overturned bulk of the animal he had slain. His mighty bow was in his hand. As Howard watched in awe, Gilgamesh aimed and let fly. The shaft struck the nearest horseman, traveling through jerkin and rib cage and all, and emerging from the man's back. But still the onrushing warrior managed to release one last arrow before he fell. It traveled on an erratic trajectory, humming quickly toward Gilgamesh on a wild wobbly arc and skewering him through the flesh of his left forearm.

Coolly the Sumerian glanced down at the arrow jutting from his arm. He scowled and shook his head, the way he might if he had been stung by a hornet. Then—as Conan might have done, how very much like Conan!—Gilgamesh inclined his head toward his shoulder and bit the arrow in half just below the fletching. Bright blood spouted from the wound as he pulled the two pieces of the arrow from his arm.

As though nothing very significant had happened, Gilgamesh lifted his bow and reached for a second shaft. Blood was streaming in rivulets down his arm, but he seemed not even to be aware of it.

Howard watched as if in a stupor. He could not move; he barely had the will to draw breath. A haze of nausea threatened to overwhelm him. It had been nothing at all for him to heap up great bloody mounds of severed heads and arms and legs with cheerful abandon in his stories; but in fact, real bloodshed and violence of any sort had horrified him whenever he had even a glimpse of it.

"The gun, Bob!" said Lovecraft urgently beside him. "Use the gun!"

"What?"

"There. There."

Howard looked down. Thrust through his belt was the pistol he had taken from the Land Rover when he had come out to investigate that little beast in the road. He drew it now and stared at it, glassy-eyed, as though it were a basilisk's egg that rested on the palm of his hand.

"What are you doing?" Lovecraft asked. "Ah. Ah. Give it to me." He snatched the gun impatiently from Howard's frozen fingers and studied it a moment as though he had never held a weapon before. Perhaps he never had. But then, grasping the pistol with both his hands, he rose warily above the hood of the Land Rover and squeezed off a shot.

The tremendous sound of an explosion cut through the shrill cries of the horsemen. Lovecraft laughed. "Got one! Who would ever have imagined—"

He fired again. In the same moment Gilgamesh brought down one more of the attackers with his bow.

"They're backing off!" Lovecraft cried. "By Alhazred, they didn't expect this, I wager!" He laughed again and poked the gun up into a firing position. "Ia!" he cried, in a voice Howard had never heard out of the shy and scholarly Lovecraft before. "Shub-Niggurath!" Lovecraft fired a third time. "Ph'nglui mglw'nafh Cthulhu R'lyeh wgah'nagl fhtagn!"

Howard felt sweat rolling down his body. This inaction of his—this paralysis, this shame—what would Conan make of it? What would Gilgamesh? And Lovecraft, that timid and sheltered man, he who dreaded the fishes of the sea and the cold winds of his New England winters and so many other things, was laughing and bellowing his wondrous gibberish and blazing away like any gangster, having the time of his life—

Shame! Shame!

Heedless of the risk, Howard scrambled up into the cab of the Land Rover and groped around for the second gun that was lying down there on the floor somewhere. He found it and knelt beside the window. Seven or eight of the Asiatic horsemen lay strewn about, dead or dying, within a hundred-yard radius of the car. The others had withdrawn to a considerable distance and were cantering in uneasy circles. They appeared taken aback by the unexpectedly fierce resistance they had encountered on what they had probably expected to have been an easy bit of jolly slaughter in these untracked frontierlands.

What were they doing now? Drawing together, a tight little ground, horses nose to nose. Conferring. And now two of them were pulling what seemed to be some sort of war-banner from a saddlebag and hoisting it between them on bamboo poles: a long yellow streamer with fluttering blood-red tips, on which bold Oriental characters were painted in shining black. Serious business, obviously. Now they were lining themselves up in a row, facing the Land Rover. Getting ready for a desperate suicide charge—that was the way things appeared.

Gilgamesh, standing erect in full view, calmly nocked yet another arrow. He took aim and waited for them to come.

Lovecraft, looking flushed with excitement, wholly transformed by the alien joys of armed combat, was leaning forward, staring intently, his pistol cocked and ready.

Howard shivered. Shame rode him with burning spurs. How could he cower here while those two bore the brunt of the struggle? Though his hand was shaking, he thrust the pistol out the window and drew a bead on the closest horseman. His finger tightened on the trigger. Would it be possible to score a hit at such a distance? Yes. Yes. Go ahead. You know how to use a gun, all right. High time you put some of that skill to use. Knock that little yellow bastard off his horse with one bark of the Colt .380, yes. Send him straight to Hell—no, he's in Hell already, send him off to the Undertaker for recycling. Yes, that's it. Ready—aim—

"Wait," Lovecraft said. "Don't shoot."

What was this? As Howard, with an effort, lowered his gun and let his rigid quivering hand go slack, Lovecraft, shading his eyes against the eerie glare of the motionless sun, peered closely at the enemy warriors a long silent moment. Then he turned, reached up into the rear of the Land Rover, groped around for a moment, finally pulled out the manila envelope that held their royal commission from King Henry.

And then—what was he doing?

Stepping out into plain view, arms raised high, waving the envelope around, walking toward the enemy?

"They'll kill you, H.P.! Get down! Get down!"

Lovecraft, without looking back, gestured brusquely for Howard to be silent. He continued to walk steadily toward the far-off horsemen. They seemed just as mystified as Howard was. They sat without moving, their bows held stiffly out before them, a dozen arrows trained on the middle of Lovecraft's body.

He's gone completely off the deep end, Howard thought in dismay. He never was really well balanced, was he? Half believing all his stuff about Elder Gods and dimensional gateways and blasphemous rites on dark New England hillsides. And now all this shooting—the excitement—

"Hold your weapons, all of you!" Lovecraft cried in a voice of amazing strength and presence. "In the name of Prester John, I bid you hold your weapons! We are not your enemies! We are ambassadors to your emperor!"

Howard gasped. He began to understand. No, Lovecraft hadn't gone crazy after all!

He took another look at that long yellow war-banner. Yes, yes, it bore the emblems of Prester John! These berserk horsemen must be part of the border patrol of the very nation whose ruler they had traveled so long to find. Howard felt abashed, realizing that in the fury of the battle Lovecraft had had the sense actually to pause long enough to give the banner's legend close examination—and the courage to walk out there waving his diplomatic credentials. The parchment scroll of their royal commission was in his hand, and he was pointing to the little red-ribboned seal of King Henry.

The horsemen stared, muttered among themselves, lowered their bows. Gilgamesh, lowering his great bow also, looked on in puzzlement. “Do you see?” Lovecraft called. “We are heralds of King Henry! We claim the protection of your master the August Sovereign Yeh-lu Ta-shih!” Glancing back over his shoulder, he called to Howard to join him; and after only an instant’s hesitation, Howard leaped down from the Land Rover and trotted forward. It was a giddy feeling, exposing himself to those somber yellow archers this way. It felt almost like standing on the edge of some colossal precipice.

Lovecraft smiled. “It’s all going to be all right, Bob! That banner they unfurled, it bears the markings of Prester John—”

“Yes, yes. I see.”

“And look—they’re making a safe-conduct sign. They understand what I’m saying, Bob! They believe me!”

Howard nodded. He felt a great upsurge of relief and even a sort of joy. He clapped Lovecraft lustily on the back. “Fine going, H.P.! I didn’t think you had it in you!” Coming up out of his funk, now, he felt a manic exuberance seize his spirit. He gestured to the horsemen, wigwagging his arms with wild vigor. “Hoy! Royal commissioners!” he bellowed. “Envoys from His Britannic Majesty King Henry VIII! Take us to your emperor!” Then he looked toward Gilgamesh, who stood frowning, his bow still at the ready. “Hoy there, king of

Uruk! Put away the weapons! Everything's all right now! We're going to be escorted to the court of Prester John!"

* * * *

Gilgamesh wasn't at all sure why he had let himself go along. He had no interest in visiting Prester John's court, or anybody else's. He wanted nothing more than to be left alone to hunt and roam in the wilderness and thereby to find some ease for his sorrows.

But the gaunt long-necked man and his blustery red-faced friend had beckoned him to ride with them in their Land Rover, and while he stood there frowning over that, the ugly flat-featured little yellow warriors had indicated with quick impatient gestures that he should get in. And he had. They looked as though they would try to compel him to get in if he balked; and though he had no fear of them, none whatever, some impulse that he could not begin to understand had led him to step back from the likelihood of yet another battle and simply climb aboard the vehicle. Perhaps he had had enough of solitary hunting for a while. Or perhaps it was just that the wound in his arm was beginning to throb and ache, now that the excitement of the fray was receding, and it seemed like a good idea to have it looked after by a surgeon. The flesh all around it was badly swollen and bruised. That arrow had pierced him through and through. He would have the wound cleaned and dressed, and then he would move along.

Well, then, so he was going to the court of Prester John. Here he was, sitting back silent and somber in the rear of this musty, mildew-flecked car, riding with these two very odd New Dead types, these scribes or tale-tellers or whatever it was they claimed to be, as the horsemen of Prester John led them to the encampment of their monarch.

The one who called himself Howard, the one who could not help stealing sly little glances at him like an infatuated schoolgirl, was at the wheel. Glancing back at his passenger now, he said, "Tell me, Gilgamesh: have you had dealings with Prester John before?"

"I have heard the name, that much I know," replied the Sumerian. "But it means little to me."

"The legendary Christian emperor," said the other, the thin one, Lovecraft. "He who was said to rule a secret kingdom somewhere in the misty hinterlands of Central Asia—although it was in Africa, according to some—"

Asia, Africa—names, only names, Gilgamesh thought bleakly. They were places somewhere in the other world, but he had no idea where they might be.

Such a multitude of places, so many names! It was impossible to keep it all straight. There was no sense of any of it. The world—his world, the Land—had been bordered by the Two Rivers, the Idigna and the Buranunu, which the Greeks had preferred to call the Tigris and the Euphrates. Who were the Greeks, and by what right had they renamed the rivers? Everyone used those names now, even Gilgamesh himself, except in the inwardness of his soul.

And beyond the Two Rivers? Why, there was the vassal state of Aratta far to the east, and in that direction also lay the Land of Cedars, where the fire-breathing demon Huwawa roared and bellowed, and in the eastern mountains lay the kingdom of the barbaric Elamites. To the north was the land called Uri, and in the deserts of the west the wild Martu people dwelled, and in the south was the blessed isle Dilmun, which was like a paradise. Was there anything more to the world than that? Why, there was Meluhha far away beyond Elam, where the people had black skins and fine features, and there was Punt in the south, where they were black also, with flat noses and thick lips. And there was another land even beyond Meluhha, with folk of yellow skins who mined a precious green stone. And that was the world. Where could all these other latter-day places be—this Africa and this Asia and Europe and the rest, Rome, Greece, England? Perhaps some of them were mere new names for old places. The Land itself had had a host of names since his own time—Babylonia, Mesopotamia, Iraq, and more. Why had it needed all those names? He had no idea. New men made up new names: that seemed to be the way of the world. This Africa, this Asia—America, China, Russia. A little man named Herodotus, a Greek, had tried to explain it all to him once—the shape of the world and the names of the places in it, sketching a map for him on an old bit of parchment—and much later a stolid fellow named Mercator had done the same, and once after that he had spoken of such matters with an Englishman called Cook; but the things they told him all conflicted with one another and he could make no sense out of any of it. It was too much to ask, making sense of these things. Those myriad nations that had arisen after his time, those empires that had arisen and fallen and been forgotten, all those lost dynasties, the captains and the kings—he had tried from time to time to master the sequence of them, but it was no use. Once in his former life he had sought to make himself the master of all knowledge, yes. His appetites had been boundless: for knowledge, for wealth, for power, for women, for life itself. Now all that seemed only the merest folly to him. That jumble of confused and confusing places, all those great realms and far-off kingdoms, were in another world: what could they matter to him now?

"Asia?" he said. "Africa?" Gilgamesh shrugged. "Prester John?" He prowled the turbulent cluttered recesses of his memory. "Ah. There's a Prester John, I think, lives in New Hell. A dark-skinned man, a friend of that gaudy old liar Sir John Mandeville." It was coming back now. "Yes, I've seen them together many times, in that dirty squalid tavern where Mandeville's always to be found. The two of them telling outlandish stories back and forth, each a bigger fraud than the other."

"A different Prester John," said Lovecraft.

"That one is Susenyos the Ethiop, I think," Howard said. "A former African tyrant, and lover of the Jesuits, now far gone in whiskey. He's one of many. There are seven, nine, a dozen Prester Johns in Hell, to my certain knowledge. And maybe more."

Gilgamesh contemplated that notion blankly. Fire was running up and down his injured arm now.

Lovecraft was saying, "—not a true name, but merely a title, and a corrupt one at that. There never was a real Prester John, only various rulers in various distant places, whom it pleased the tale-spinners of Europe to speak of as Prester John, the Christian emperor, the great mysterious unknown monarch of a fabulous realm. And here in Hell there are many who choose to wear the name. There's power in it, do you see?"

"Power and majesty!" Howard cried. "And poetry, by God!"

"So this Prester John whom we are to visit," said Gilgamesh, "he is not in fact Prester John?"

"Yeh-lu Ta-shih's his name," said Howard. "Chinese. Manchurian, actually, twelfth century A.D. First emperor of the realm of Kara-Khitai, with his capital at Samarkand. Ruled over a bunch of Mongols and Turks, mainly, and they called him Gur Khan, which means 'supreme ruler,' and somehow that turned into 'John' by the time it got to Europe. And they said he was a Christian priest, too, Presbyter Joannes, 'Prester John.'" Howard laughed. "Damned silly bastards. He was no more a Christian than you were. A Buddhist, he was, a bloody shamanistic Buddhist."

"Then why—"

"Myth and confusion!" Howard said. "The great human nonsense factory at work! And wouldn't you know it, but when he got to Hell this Yeh-lu Ta-shih founded himself another empire right away in the same sort of territory he'd lived in back there, and when Richard Burton came out this way and told him about Prester John and how Europeans long ago had spoken of him by that name and ascribed all sorts of fabulous accomplishments to him he said, 'Yes, yes, I am Prester John indeed.' And so he styles himself that way now, he and nine or ten others, most of them Ethiopians like that friend of your friend Mandeville."

"They are no friends of mine," said Gilgamesh stiffly. He leaned back and massaged his aching arm. Outside the Land Rover the landscape was changing now: more hilly, with ill-favored fat-trunked little trees jutting at peculiar angles from the purple soil. Here and there in the distance his keen eyes made out scattered groups of black tents on the hillsides, and herds of the little Hell-horses grazing near them. Gilgamesh wished now that he hadn't let himself be inveigled into this expedition. What need had he of Prester John? One of these upstart New Dead potentates, one of the innumerable little princelings who had set up minor dominions for themselves out here in the vast measureless wastelands of the Outback—and reigning under a false name, at that—one more shoddy scoundrel, one more puffed-up little nobody swollen with unearned pride—

Well, and what difference did it make? He would sojourn a while in the land of this Prester John, and then he would move on, alone, apart from others, mourning as always his lost Enkidu. There seemed no escaping that doom that lay upon him, that bitter solitude, whether he reigned in splendor in Uruk or wandered in the wastes of Hell.

* * * *

"Their Excellencies P.E. Lovecraft and Howard E. Robert," cried the major-domo grandly though inaccurately, striking three times on the black marble floor of Prester John's throne-chamber with his gold-tipped staff of pale green jade. "Envoys Plenipotentiary of His Britannic Majesty King Henry VIII of the Kingdom of New Holy Diabolic England."

Lovecraft and Howard took a couple of steps forward. Yeh-lu Ta-shih nodded curtly and waved one elegant hand, resplendent with inch-long fingernails, in casual acknowledgment. The envoys plenipotentiary did not seem to hold much interest for him, nor, apparently, did whatever it was that had caused His Britannic Majesty King Henry to send them here.

The emperor's cool imperious glance turned toward Gilgamesh, who was struggling to hold himself erect. He was beginning to feel feverish and dizzy and he wondered when anyone would notice that there was an oozing hole in his arm. Even he had limits to his endurance, after all, though he usually tried to conceal that fact. He didn't know how much longer he could hold out. There were times when behaving like a hero was a heroic pain in the ass, and this was one of them.

"—and his Late Highness Gilgamesh of Uruk, son of Lugalbanda, great king, king of Uruk, king of kings, lord of the Land of the Two Rivers by merit of Enlil and An," boomed the major-domo in the same splendid way, looking down only once at the card he held in his hand.

"Great king?" said Yeh-lu Ta-shih, fixing Gilgamesh with one of the most intensely penetrating stares the Sumerian could remember ever having received. "King of kings? Those are very lofty titles, Gilgamesh of Uruk."

"A mere formula," Gilgamesh replied, "which I thought appropriate when being presented at your court. In fact I am king of nothing at all now."

"Ah," said Yeh-lu Ta-shih. "King of Nothing-at-all."

And so are you, my lord Prester John. Gilgamesh did not let himself say it, though the words bubbled toward the roof of his mouth and begged to be uttered. And so are all the self-appointed lords and masters of the many realms of Hell.

The slender amber-hued man on the throne leaned forward. "And where then, I pray, is Nothing-at-all?"

Some of the courtiers began to snicker. But Prester John looked to be altogether in earnest, though it was impossible to be completely certain of that. He was plainly a formidable man, Gilgamesh had quickly come to see: sly, shrewd, self-contained, with a tough and sinewy intelligence. Not at all the vain little cock-of-the-walk Gilgamesh had expected to find in this bleak and remote corner of Hell. However small and obscure his principality might be, Prester John ruled it, obviously, with a firm grasp. The grandeur of the glittering palace that his scruffy subjects had built for him here on the edge of nowhere, and the solidity of the small but substantial city surrounding it, testified to that. Gilgamesh knew something about the building of cities and palaces. Prester John's capital bore the mark of the steady toil of centuries.

The long stare was unrelenting. Gilgamesh, fighting back the blazing pain in his arm, met the emperor's gaze with an equally earnest one of his own and said:

"Nothing-at-all? It is a land that never was, and will always be, my lord. Its boundaries are nowhere and its capital city is everywhere, nor do any of us ever leave it."

"Ah. Ah. Indeed. Nicely put. You are Old Dead, are you?"

"Very old, my lord."

"Older than Ch'in Shih Huang Ti? Older than the Lords of Shang and Hsia?"

Gilgamesh turned in puzzlement toward Lovecraft, who told him in a half-whisper, "Ancient kings of China. Your time was even earlier."

Shrugging, Gilgamesh replied, "They are not known to me, my lord, but you hear what the Britannic ambassador says. He is a man of learning: it must be so. I will tell you that I am older than Caesar by far, older than Agamemnon and the Supreme Commander Rameses, older even than Sargon. By a great deal."

Yeh-lu Ta-shih considered that a moment. Then he made another of his little gestures of dismissal, as though brushing aside the whole concept of relative ages in Hell. With a dry laugh he said, "So you are very old, King Gilgamesh. I congratulate you. And yet the Ice-Hunter folk would tell us that you and I and Rameses and Sargon all arrived here only yesterday; and to the Hairy Men, the Ice-Hunters themselves are mere newcomers. And so on and so on. There's no beginning to it, is there? Any more than there's an end."

Without waiting for an answer he asked Gilgamesh, "How did you come by that gory wound, great king of Nothing-at-all?"

At least he's noticed it, Gilgamesh thought.

"A misunderstanding, my lord. It may be that your border patrol is a little overzealous at times."

One of the courtiers leaned toward the emperor and murmured something. Prester John's serene brow grew furrowed. He lifted a flawlessly contoured eyebrow ever so slightly.

"Killed nine of them, did you?"

"They attacked us before we had the opportunity of showing our diplomatic credentials," Lovecraft put in quickly. "It was entirely a matter of self-defense, my lord Prester John."

"I wouldn't doubt it." The emperor seemed to contemplate for a moment, but only for a moment, the skirmish that had cost the lives of nine of his horsemen; and then quite visibly he dismissed that matter too from the center of his attention. "Well, now, my lords ambassador—"

Abruptly Gilgamesh swayed, tottered, started to fall. He checked himself just barely in time, seizing a massive porphyry column and clinging to it until he felt more steady. Beads of sweat trickled down his forehead into his eyes. He began to shiver. The huge stone column seemed to be expanding and contracting. Waves of vertigo were rippling through him and he was seeing double, suddenly. Everything was blurring and multiplying. He drew his breath in deeply, again, again, forcing himself to hold on. He wondered if Prester John was playing some kind of game with him, trying to see how long his strength could last. Well, if he had to, Gilgamesh swore, he would stand here forever in front of Prester John without showing a hint of weakness.

But now Yeh-lu Ta-shih was at last willing to extend compassion. With a glance toward one of his pages the emperor said, "Summon my physician, and tell him to bring his tools and his potions. That wound should have been dressed an hour ago."

"Thank you, my lord," Gilgamesh muttered, trying to keep the irony from his tone.

The doctor appeared almost at once, as though he had been waiting in an antechamber. Another of Prester John's little games, perhaps? He was a burly, broad-shouldered, bushy-haired man of more than middle years, with a manner about him that was brisk and bustling but nevertheless warm, concerned, reassuring. Drawing Gilgamesh down beside him on a low divan covered with the gray-green hide of some scaly Hell-dragon, he peered into the wound, muttered something unintelligible to himself in a guttural language unknown to the Sumerian, and pressed his thick fingers around the edges of the torn flesh until fresh blood flowed. Gilgamesh hissed sharply but did not flinch.

"Ach, mein lieber Freund, I must hurt you again, but it is for your own good. Verstehen sie?"

The doctor's fingers dug in more deeply. He was spreading the wound, swabbing it, cleansing it with some clear fluid that stung like a hot iron. The pain was so intense that there was almost a kind of pleasure in it: it was a purifying kind of pain, a purging of the soul.

Prester John said, "How bad is it, Dr. Schweitzer?"

"Gott sei dank, it is deep but clean. He will heal without damage."

He continued to probe and cleanse; murmuring softly to Gilgamesh as he worked: "Bitte. Bitte. Einen Augenblick, mein Freund." To Prester John he said, "This man is made of steel. No nerves at all, immense resistance to pain. We have one of the great heroes here, nicht wahr? You are Roland, are you? Achilles, perhaps?"

"Gilgamesh is his name," said Yeh-lu Ta-shih.

The doctor's eyes grew bright. "Gilgamesh! Gilgamesh of Sumer? Wunderbar! Wunderbar! The very man. The seeker after life. Ach, we must talk, my friend, you and I, when you are feeling better." From his medical kit he now produced a frightful-looking hypodermic syringe. Gilgamesh watched as though from a vast distance, as though that throbbing swollen arm belonged to someone else. "Ja, ja, certainly we must talk, of life, of death, or philosophy, mein Freund, of philosophy! There is so very much for us to discuss!" He slipped the needle beneath Gilgamesh's skin. "There. Genug. Sit. Rest. The healing now begins."

* * * *

Robert Howard had never seen anything like it. It could have been something straight from the pages of one of his Conan stories. The big ox had taken an arrow right through the fat part of his arm, and he had simply yanked it out and gone right on fighting. Then, afterward, he had behaved as if the wound were nothing more than a scratch, all that time while they were driving hour after hour toward Prester John's city and then undergoing lengthy interrogation by the court officials and then standing through this whole endless ceremony at court—God almighty, what a display of endurance! True, Gilgamesh had finally gone a little wobbly and had actually seemed on the verge of passing out. But any ordinary mortal would have conked out long ago. Heroes really were different. They were another breed altogether. Look at him now, sitting there casually while that old

German medic swabs him out and stitches him up in that slapdash cavalier way, and not a whimper out of him. Not a whimper!

Suddenly Howard found himself wanting to go over there to Gilgamesh, to comfort him, to let him lean his head back against him while the doctor worked him over, to wipe the sweat from his brow—

Yes, to comfort him in an open, rugged, manly way—

No. No. No. No.

There it was again, the horror, the unspeakable thing, the hideous crawling Hell-borne impulse rising out of the cesspools of his soul—

Howard fought it back. Blotted it out, hid it from view. Denied that it had ever entered his mind.

To Lovecraft he said, "That's some doctor! Took his medical degree at the Chicago slaughterhouses, I reckon!"

"Don't you know who he is, Bob?"

"Some old Dutchman who wandered in here during a sandstorm and never bothered to leave."

"Does the name Dr. Schweitzer mean nothing to you?"

Howard gave Lovecraft a blank look. "Guess I never heard it much in Texas."

"Oh, Bob, Bob, why must you always pretend to be such a cowboy? Can you tell me you've never heard of Schweitzer? Albert Schweitzer? The great philosopher, theologian, musician—there never was a greater interpreter of Bach, and don't tell me you don't know Bach either—"

"She-it, H.P., you talking about that old country doctor there?"

"Who founded the leprosy clinic in Africa, at Lambarene, yes. Who devoted his life to helping the sick, under the most primitive conditions, in the most remote forests of—"

"Hold on, H.P. That can't be so."

"That one man could achieve so much? I assure you, Bob, he was quite well known in our time—perhaps not in Texas, I suppose, but nevertheless—"

"No. Not that he could do all that. But that he's here. In Hell. If that old geezer's everything you say, then he's a goddamned saint. Unless he beat his wife when no one was looking, or something like that. What's a saint doing in Hell, H.P.?"

"What are we doing in Hell?" Lovecraft asked.

Howard reddened and looked away. "Well, I suppose, there were things in our lives—things that might be considered sins, in the strictest sense—"

"No one understands the rules of Hell, Bob," said Lovecraft gently. "Sin may have nothing to do with it. Gandhi is here, do you realize that? Confucius. Were they sinners? Was Moses? Abraham? We've tried to impose our own pitiful shallow beliefs, our pathetic grade-school notions of punishment for bad behavior, on this incredibly bizarre place where we find ourselves. By what right? We don't begin to comprehend what Hell really is. All we know is that it's full of heroic villains and villainous heroes—and people like you and me—and it seems that Albert Schweitzer is here, too. A great mystery. But perhaps someday—"

"Shh," Howard said. "Prester John's talking to us."

"My lords ambassador—"

Hastily they turned toward him. "Your majesty?" Howard said.

"This mission that has brought you here: your king wants an alliance, I suppose? What for? Against whom? Quarreling with some pope again, is he?"

"With his daughter, I'm afraid," said Howard.

Prester John looked bored. He toyed with his emerald scepter. "Mary, you mean?"

"Elizabeth, your majesty," Lovecraft said.

"Your king's a most quarrelsome man. I'd have thought there were enough popes in Hell to keep him busy, though, and no need to contend with his daughters."

"They are the most contentious women in Hell," Lovecraft said. "Blood of his blood, after all, and each of them a queen with a noisy, brawling kingdom of her own. Elizabeth, my lord, is sending a pack of her explorers to the Outback, and King Henry doesn't like the idea."

"Indeed," said Yeh-lu Ta-shih, suddenly interested again. "And neither do I. She has no business in the Outback. It's not her territory. The rest of Hell should be big enough for Elizabeth. What is she looking for here?"

"The sorcerer John Dee has told her that the way out of Hell is to be found in these parts."

"There is no way out of Hell."

Lovecraft smiled. "I'm not any judge of that, your majesty. Queen Elizabeth, in any event, has given credence to the notion. Her Walter Raleigh directs the expedition, and the geographer Hakluyt is with him, and a force of five hundred soldiers. They move diagonally across the Outback just to the south of your domain, following some chart that Dr. Dee had obtained for them. He had it from Cagliostro, they say, who bought it from Hadrian when Hadrian was still supreme commander of Hell's legions. It is allegedly an official Satanic document."

Prester John did not appear to be impressed. "Let us say, for argument's sake, that there is an exit from Hell. Why would Queen Elizabeth desire to leave? Hell's not so bad. It has its minor discomforts, yes, but one learns to cope with them. Does she think she'd be able to reign in Heaven as she does here—assuming there's a Heaven at all, which is distinctly not proven?"

"Elizabeth has no real interest in leaving Hell herself, majesty," Howard said. "What King Henry fears is that if she does find the way out, she'll claim it for her own and set up a colony around it, and charge a fee for passing through the gate. No matter where it takes you, the king reckons there'll be millions of people willing to risk it, and Elizabeth will wind up cornering all the money in Hell. He can't abide that notion, d'ye see? He thinks she's already too smart and aggressive by half, and he hates the idea that she might get even more powerful. There's something mixed into it having to do with Queen Elizabeth's mother, too—that was Anne Boleyn, Henry's second wife. She was a wild and wanton one, and he cut her head off for adultery, and now he thinks that Anne's behind Elizabeth's maneuvers, trying to get even with him by—"

"Spare me these details," said Yeh-lu Ta-shih with some irritation. "What does Henry expect me to do?"

"Send troops to turn the Raleigh expedition back before it can find anything useful to Elizabeth."

"And in what way do I gain from this?"

"If the exit from Hell's on your frontier, your majesty, do you really want a bunch of Elizabethan Englishmen setting up a colony next door to you?"

"There is no exit from Hell," Prester John said complacently once again.

"But if they set up a colony anyway?"

Prester John was silent a moment. "I see," he said finally.

"In return for your aid," Howard said, "we're empowered to offer you a trade treaty on highly favorable terms."

"Ah."

"And a guarantee of military protection in the event of the invasion of your realm by a hostile power."

"If King Henry's armies are so mighty, why does he not deal with the Raleigh expedition himself?"

"There was no time to outfit and dispatch an army across such a great distance," said Lovecraft. "Elizabeth's people had already set out before anything was known of the scheme."

"Ah," said Yeh-lu Ta-shih.

"Of course," Lovecraft went on, "there were other princes of the Outback that King Henry might have approached. Moammar Khadafy's name came up, and one of the Assyrians—Assurnasirpal, I think—and someone mentioned Mao Tse-tung. No, King Henry said, let us ask the aid of Prester John, for he is a monarch of great puissance and grandeur, whose writ is supreme throughout the far reaches of Hell. Prester John, indeed, that is the one whose aid we must seek!"

A strange new sparkle had come into Yeh-lu Ta-shih's eyes. "You were considering an alliance with Mao Tse-tung?"

"It was merely a suggestion, your majesty."

"Ah. I see." The emperor rose from his throne. "Well, we must consider these matters more carefully, eh? We must not come hastily to a decision." He looked across the great vaulted throne room to the divan where Dr. Schweitzer still labored over Gilgamesh's wound. "Your patient, doctor—what's the report?"

"A man of steel, majesty, a man of steel! Gott sei dank, he heals before my eyes!"

"Indeed. Come, then. You will all want to rest, I think; and then you shall know the full hospitality of Prester John."

* * * *

The full hospitality of Prester John, Gilgamesh soon discovered, was no trifling affair.

He was led off to a private chamber with walls lined with black felt—a kind of indoor tent—where three serving-girls who stood barely hip-high to him surrounded him, giggling, and took his clothing from him. Gently they pushed him into a huge marble cistern full of warm milk, where they bathed him lovingly and massaged his aching body in the most intimate manner. Afterward they robed him in intricate vestments of yellow silk.

Then they conveyed him to the emperor's great hall, where the whole court was gathered, a glittering and resplendent multitude. Some sort of concert was under way, seven solemn musicians playing harsh screeching twanging music. Gongs crashed, a trumpet blared, pipes uttered eerie piercing sounds. Servants showed Gilgamesh to a place of honor atop a pile of furry blankets heaped high with velvet cushions.

Lovecraft and Howard were already there, garbed like Gilgamesh in magnificent silks. Both of them looked somewhat unsettled—unhinged, even. Howard, flushed and boisterous, could barely sit still: he laughed and waved his arms and kicked his heels against the furs, like a small boy who has done something very naughty and is trying to conceal it by being over-exuberant. Lovecraft, on the other hand, seemed dazed and dislocated, with the glassy-eyed look of someone who has recently been clubbed.

These are two very odd men indeed, Gilgamesh thought.

One works hard at being loud and lusty, and now and then gives you a glimpse of a soul boiling with wild fantasies of swinging swords and rivers of blood. But in reality he seems terrified of everything. The other, though he is weirdly remote and austere, is apparently not quite as crazy, but he too gives the impression of being at war with himself, in terror of allowing any sort of real human feeling to break through the elaborate facade of his mannerisms. The poor fools must have been scared silly when the serving-girls started stripping them and pouring warm milk over them and stroking their bodies. No doubt they haven't recovered yet from all that nasty pleasure, Gilgamesh thought. He could imagine their cries of horror as the little Mongol girls started going to work on them. What are you doing? Leave my trousers alone! Don't touch me there! Please—no—ooh—ah—ooh! Oooh!

Yeh-lu Ta-shih, seated upon a high throne of ivory and onyx, waved grandly to him, one great king to another. Gilgamesh gave him an almost imperceptible nod by way of acknowledgment. All this pomp and formality bored him hideously. He had endured so much of it in his former life, after all. And then he had been the one on the high throne, but even then it had been nothing but a bore. And now—

But this was no more boring than anything else. Gilgamesh had long ago decided that that was the true curse of Hell: all striving was meaningless here, mere thunder without the lightning. And there was no end to it. You might die again now and then if you were careless or unlucky, but back you came for another turn, sooner or later, at the Undertaker's whim. There was no release from the everlastingness of it all. Once he had yearned desperately for eternal life, and he had learned that he could not have such a thing, at least not in the world of mortal men. But now indeed he had come to a place where he would live forever, so it seemed, and yet there was no joy in it. His fondest dream now was simply to serve his time in Hell and be allowed to sleep in peace forever. He saw no way of attaining that. Life here just went on and on—very much like this concert, this endless skein of twangs and plinks and screeches.

Someone with the soft face of a eunuch came by and offered him a morsel of grilled meat. Gilgamesh knew he would pay for it later—you always did, when you ate something in Hell—but he was hungry now, and he gobbled it. And another, and another, and a flagon of fermented mare's milk besides.

A corps of dancers appeared, men and women in flaring filmy robes. They were doing things with swords and flaming torches. A second eunuch brought Gilgamesh a tray of mysterious sugary delicacies, and he helped himself with both hands, heedless of the consequences. He was ravenous. His body, as it healed, was calling furiously for fuel. Beside him, the man Howard was swilling down the mare's milk as if it were water and getting tipsier and tipsier, and the other, the one called Lovecraft, sat morosely staring at the dancers without touching a thing. He seemed to be shivering as though in the midst of a snowstorm.

Gilgamesh beckoned for a second flagon. Just then the doctor arrived and settled down cheerfully on the heap of blankets next to him. Schweitzer grinned his approval as Gilgamesh took a hearty drink. “Fuhlen Sie sich besser, mein Held, eh? The arm, it no longer gives you pain? Already the wound is closing. So quickly you repair yourself! Such strength, such power and healing! You are God’s own miracle, dear Gilgamesh. The blessing of the Almighty is upon you.” He seized a flagon of his own from a passing servant, quaffed it, made a face. “Ach, this milk-wine of theirs! And ach, ach, this verfluchte music! What I would give for the taste of decent Moselle on my tongue now, eh, and the sound of the D minor toccata and fugue in my ears! Bach—do you know him?”

“Who?”

“Bach! Bach, Johann Sebastian Bach. The greatest of musicians, God’s own poet in sound. I saw him once, just once, years ago.” Schweitzer’s eyes were glowing. “I was new here. Not two weeks had I been here. It was at the villa of King Friedrich—Frederick the Great, you know him? No? The king of Prussia? Der alte Fritz? No matter. No matter. Er macht nichts. A man entered, ordinary, you would never notice him in a crowd, yes? And began to play the harpsichord, and he had not played three measures when I said, 'This is Bach, this must be the actual Bach,' and I would have dropped down on my knees before him but that I was ashamed. And it was he. I said to myself, 'Why is it that Bach is in Hell?' But then I said, as perhaps you have said, as I think everyone here must say at one time or another, 'Why is it that Schweitzer is in Hell?' And I knew that it is that God is mysterious. Perhaps I was sent here to minister to the damned. Perhaps it is that Bach was also. Or perhaps we are damned also; or perhaps no one here is damned. Es macht nichts aus, all this speculation. It is a mistake, or even vielleicht a sin, to imagine that we can comprehend the workings of the mind of God. We are here. We have our tasks. That is enough for me to know."

"I felt that way once," said Gilgamesh. "When I was king in Uruk, and finally came to understand that I must die, that there was no hiding from that. What is the purpose, then, I asked myself? And I told myself: The gods have put us here to perform our tasks, and that is the purpose. And so I lived thereafter and so I died." Gilgamesh's face darkened. "But here—here—"

"Here, too, we have our tasks," Schweitzer said.

"You do, perhaps. For me there is only the task of passing the time. I had a friend to bear the burden with me once—"

"Enkidu."

Gilgamesh seized the doctor's sturdy wrist with sudden fierce intensity. "You know of Enkidu?"

"From the poem, yes. The poem is very famous."

"Ah. Ah. The poem. But the actual man—"

"I know nothing of him, nein."

"He is of my stature, very large. His beard is thick, his hair is shaggy, his shoulders are wider even than mine. We journeyed everywhere together. But then we quarreled, and he went from me in anger, saying, 'Never cross my path again.' Saying, 'I have no love for you, Gilgamesh.' Saying, 'If we meet again I will have your life.' And I have heard nothing of him since."

Schweitzer turned and stared closely at Gilgamesh. "How is this possible? All the world knows the love of Enkidu for Gilgamesh!"

Gilgamesh called for yet another flagon. This conversation was awakening an ache within his breast, an ache that made the pain that his wound had caused seem like nothing more than an itch. Nor would the drink soothe it; but he would drink all the same.

He took a deep draught and said somberly, "We quarreled. There were hot words between us. He said he had no love for me any longer."

"This cannot be true."

Gilgamesh shrugged and made no reply.

"You wish to find him again?" Schweitzer asked.

"I desire nothing else."

"Do you know where he is?"

"Hell is larger even than the world. He could be anywhere."

"You will find him."

"If you knew how I have searched for him—"

"You will find him. That I know."

Gilgamesh shook his head. "If Hell is a place of torment, then this is mine, that I will never find him again. Or if I do, that he will spurn me. Or raise his hand against me."

"This is not so," said Schweitzer. "I think he longs for you even as you do for him."

"Then why does he keep himself from me?"

"This is Hell," said Schweitzer gently. "You are being tested, my friend, but no test lasts forever. Not even in Hell. Not even in Hell. Even though you are in Hell, have faith in the Lord: You will have your Enkidu soon enough, um Himmels Willen." Smiling, Schweitzer said, "The emperor is calling you. Go to him. I think he has something to tell you that you will want to hear."

* * * *

Prester John said, "You are a warrior, are you not?"

"I was," replied Gilgamesh indifferently.

"A general? A leader of men?"

"All that is far behind me," Gilgamesh said. "This is the life after life. Now I go my own way and I take on no tasks for others. Hell has plenty of generals."

"I am told that you were a leader among leaders. I am told that you fought like the god of war. When you took the field, whole nations laid down their arms and knelt before you."

Gilgamesh waited, saying nothing.

"You miss the glory of the battlefield, don't you, Gilgamesh?"

"Do I?"

"What if I were to offer you the command of my army?"

"Why would you do that? What am I to you? What is your nation to me?"

"In Hell we take whatever citizenship we wish. What would you say, if I offered you the command?"

"I would tell you that you are making a great mistake."

"It isn't a trivial army. Ten thousand men. Adequate air support. Tactical nukes. The strongest firepower in the Outback."

"You misunderstand," said Gilgamesh. "Warfare doesn't interest me. I know nothing of modern weapons and don't care to learn. You have the wrong man, Prester John. If you need a general, send for Wellington. Send for Marlborough. Rommel. Tiglath-Pileser."

"Or for Enkidu?"

The unexpected name hit Gilgamesh like a battering ram. At the sound of it his face grew hot and his entire body trembled convulsively.

"What do you know about Enkidu?"

Prester John held up one superbly manicured hand. "Allow me the privilege of asking the questions, great king."

"You spoke the name of Enkidu. What do you know about Enkidu?"

"First let us discuss the matters which are of—"

"Enkidu," said Gilgamesh implacably. "Why did you mention his name?"

"I know that he was your friend—"

"Is."

"Very well, is your friend. And a man of great valor and strength. Who happens to be a guest at this very moment at the court of the great enemy of my realm. And who, so I understand it, is preparing just now to make war against me."

"What?" Gilgamesh stared. "Enkidu is in the service of Queen Elizabeth?"

"I don't recall having said that."

"Is it not Queen Elizabeth who even now has sent an army to encroach on your domain?"

Yeh-lu Ta-shih laughed. "Raleigh and his five hundred fools? That expedition's an absurdity. I'll take care of them in an afternoon. I mean another enemy altogether. Tell me this: do you know of Mao Tse-tung?"

"These princes of the New Dead—there are so many names—"

"A Chinese, a man of Han. Emperor of the Marxist Dynasty, long after my time. Crafty, stubborn, tough. More than a little crazy. He runs something called the Celestial People's Republic, just north of here. What he tells his subjects is that we can turn Hell into Heaven by collectivizing it."

"Collectivizing?" said Gilgamesh uncomprehendingly.

"To make all the peasants into kings, and the kings into peasants. As I say: more than a little crazy. But he has his hordes of loyal followers, and they do whatever he says. He means to conquer all the Outback, beginning right here. And after that, all of Hell will be subjected to his lunatic ideas. I fear that Elizabeth's in league with him—that this nonsense of looking for a way out of Hell is only a ruse, that in fact her Raleigh is spying out my weaknesses for her so that she can sell the information to Mao."

"But if this Mao is the enemy of all kings, why would Elizabeth ally herself with—"

"Obviously they mean to use each other. Elizabeth aiding Mao to overthrow me, Mao aiding Elizabeth to push her father from his throne. And then afterward, who knows? But I mean to strike before either of them can harm me."

"What about Enkidu?" Gilgamesh said. "Tell me about Enkidu."

Prester John opened a scroll of computer printout. Skimming through it, he read, "The Old Dead warrior Enkidu of Sumer—Sumer, that's your nation, isn't it?—arrived at court of Mao Tse-tung on such-and-such a date—ostensible purpose of visit, Outback hunting expedition—accompanied by American spy posing as journalist and hunter, one E. Hemingway—secret meeting with Kublai

Khan, Minister of War for the Celestial People's Republic—now training Communist troops in preparation for invasion of New Kara-Khitai—" The emperor looked up. "Is this of interest to you, Gilgamesh?"

"What is it you want from me?"

"This man is your famous friend. You know his mind as you do your own. Defend us from him and I'll give you anything you desire."

"What I desire," said Gilgamesh, "is nothing more than the friendship of Enkidu."

"Then I'll give you Enkidu on a silver platter. Take the field for me against Mao's troops. Help me anticipate whatever strategies your Enkidu has been teaching them. We'll wipe the Marxist bastards out and capture their generals, and then Enkidu will be yours. I can't guarantee that he'll want to be your friend again, but he'll be yours. What do you say, Gilgamesh? What do you say?"

* * * *

Across the gray plains of Hell from horizon to horizon sprawled the legions of Prester John. Scarlet-and-yellow banners fluttered against the somber sky. At the center of the formation stood a wedge of horseborne archers in leather armor; on each flank was a detachment of heavy infantry; the emperor's fleet of tanks was in the vanguard, rolling unhurriedly forward over the rough, broken terrain. A phalanx of transatmospheric weapons platforms provided air cover far overhead.

A cloud of dust in the distance gave evidence of the oncoming army of the Celestial People's Republic.

"By all the demons of Stygia, did you ever see such a cockeyed sight?" Robert Howard cried. He and Lovecraft had a choice view of the action from their place in the imperial command post, a splendid pagoda protected by a glowing force-shield. Gilgamesh was there, too, just across the way with Prester John and the officers of the Kara-Khitai high command. The emperor was peering into a bank of television monitors and one of his aides was feverishly tapping out orders on a computer terminal. "Makes no goddamned sense," said Howard. "Horsemen, tanks, weapons platforms, all mixing it up at the same time—is that how these wild sons of bitches fight a war?"

Lovecraft touched his forefinger to his lips. "Don't shout so, Bob. Do you want Prester John to hear you? We're his guests, remember. And King Henry's ambassadors."

"Well, if he hears me, he hears me. Look at that crazy mess! Doesn't Prester John realize that he's got a twentieth-century Bolshevik Chinaman coming to attack him with twentieth-century weapons? What good are mounted horsemen, for God's sake? A cavalry charge into the face of heavy artillery. Bows and arrows against howitzers?" Howard guffawed. "Nuclear-tipped arrows, is that the trick?"

Softly Lovecraft said, "For all we know, that's what they are."

"You know that can't be, H.P. I'm surprised at you, a man with your scientific background. I know all this nuke stuff is after our time, but surely you've kept up with the theory. Critical mass at the tip of an arrow? No, H.P., you know as well as I do that it just can't work. And even if it could—"

In exasperation Lovecraft waved to him to be silent. He pointed across the room to the main monitor in front of Prester John. The florid face of a heavyset man with a thick white beard had appeared on the screen.

"Isn't that Hemingway?" Lovecraft asked.

"Who?"

"Ernest Hemingway. The writer. A Farewell to Arms. The Sun Also Rises."

"Never could stand his stuff," said Howard. "Sick crap about a bunch of drunken weaklings. You sure that's him?"

"Weaklings, Bob?" said Lovecraft in astonishment.

"I read only the one book, about those Americans in Europe who go to the bullfights and get drunk and fool around with each other's women, and that was all of Mr. Hemingway that I cared to experience. I tell you, H.P., it disgusted me. And the way it was written! All those short little sentences—no magic, no poetry, H.P.—"

"Let's talk about it some other time, Bob."

"No vision of heroism—no awareness of the higher passions that ennoble and—"

"Bob—please—"

"A fixation on the sordid, the slimy, the depraved—"

"You're being absurd, Bob. You're completely misinterpreting his philosophy of life. If you had simply taken the trouble to read A Farewell to Arms—" Lovecraft shook his head angrily. "This is no time for a literary discussion. Look—look there." He nodded toward the far side of the room. "One of the emperor's aides is calling over. Something's going on."

Indeed there had been a development of some sort. Yeh-lu Ta-shih seemed to be conferring with four or five aides at once. Gilgamesh, red-faced, agitated, was striding swiftly back and forth in front of the computer bank. Hemingway's face was still on the screen and he too looked agitated.

Hastily Howard and Lovecraft crossed the room. The emperor turned to them. "There's been a request for a parley in the field," Prester John said, "Kublai Khan is on his way over. Dr. Schweitzer will serve as my negotiator. The man Hemingway's going to be an impartial observer—their impartial observer. I need an impartial observer, too. Will you two go down there too, as diplomats from a neutral power, to keep an eye on things?"

"An honor to serve," said Howard grandly.

"And for what purpose, my lord, has the parley been called?" Lovecraft asked.

Yeh-lu Ta-shih gestured toward the screen. "Hemingway has had the notion that we can settle this thing by single combat—Gilgamesh versus Enkidu. Save on ammunition, spare the Undertaker a devil of a lot of toil. But there's a disagreement over the details." Delicately he smothered a yawn. "Perhaps it can all be worked out by lunchtime."

* * * *

It was an oddly assorted group. Mao Tse-tung's chief negotiator was the plump, magnificently dressed Kublai Khan, whose dark sly eyes gave evidence of much cunning and force. He had been an emperor in his own right in his former life, but evidently had preferred less taxing responsibilities here. Next to him was Hemingway, big and heavy, with a deep voice and an easy, almost arrogant manner. Mao had also sent four small men in identical blue uniforms with red stars on their breasts—"Party types," someone murmured—and, strangely, a Hairy Man, big-browed and chinless, one of those creatures out of deepest antiquity. He too wore the Communist emblem on his uniform.

And there was one more to the group—the massive, deep-chested man of dark brow and fierce and smouldering eyes, who stood off by himself at the far side—

Gilgamesh could barely bring himself to look at him. He too stood apart from the group a little way, savoring the keen edge of the wind that blew across the field of battle. He longed to rush toward Enkidu, to throw his arms around him, to sweep away in one jubilant embrace all the bitterness that had separated them—

If only it could be as simple as that!

The voices of Mao's negotiators and the five that Prester John had sent—Schweitzer, Lovecraft, Howard, and a pair of Kara-Khitai officers—drifted to Gilgamesh above the howling of the wind.

Hemingway seemed to be doing most of the talking. "Writers, are you? Mr. Howard, Mr. Lovecraft? I regret I haven't had the pleasure of encountering your work."

"Fantasy, it was," said Lovecraft. "Fables. Visions."

"That so? You publish in Argosy? The Post?"

"Five to Argosy, but they were westerns," Howard said. "Mainly we wrote for Weird Tales. And H.P., a few in Astounding Stories."

"Weird Tales," Hemingway said. "Astounding Stories." A shadow of distaste flickered across his face. "Mmm. Don't think I knew those magazines. But you wrote well, did you, gentlemen? You set down what you truly felt, the real thing, and you stated it purely? Of course you did. I know you did. You were honest writers or you'd never have gone to Hell. That goes almost without saying." He laughed, rubbed his hands in glee, effusively threw his arms around the shoulders of Howard and Lovecraft. Howard seemed alarmed by that and Lovecraft looked as though he wanted to sink into the ground. "Well, gentlemen," Hemingway boomed, "what shall we do here? We have a little problem. The one hero wishes to fight with bare hands, the other with—what did he call it?—a disruptor pistol? You would know more about that than I do: something out of Astounding Stories, is how it sounds to me.

But we can't have this, can we? Bare hands against fantastic future science? There is a good way to fight and that is equal to equal, and all other ways are the bad ways."

"Let him come to me with his fists," Gilgamesh called from the distance. "As we fought the first time, in the Market-of-the-Land, when my path crossed his in Uruk."

"He is afraid to use the new weapons," Enkidu replied.

"Afraid?"

"I brought a shotgun to him, a fine 12-gauge weapon, a gift to my brother Gilgamesh. He shrank from it as though I had given him a venomous serpent."

"Lies!" roared Gilgamesh. "I had no fear of it! I despised it because it was cowardly!"

"He fears anything which is new," said Enkidu. "I never thought Gilgamesh of Uruk would know fear, but he fears the unfamiliar. He called me a coward, because I would hunt with a shotgun. But I think he was the coward. And now he fears to fight me with the unfamiliar. He knows that I'll slay him. He fears death even here, do you know that? Death has always been his great terror. Why is that? Because it is an insult to his pride? I think that is it. Too proud to die—too proud to accept the decree of the gods—"

"I will break you with my hands alone!" Gilgamesh bellowed.

"Give us disruptors," said Enkidu. "Let us see if he dares to touch such a weapon."

"A coward's weapon!"

"Again you call me a coward? You, Gilgamesh, you are the one who quivers in fear—"

"Gentlemen! Gentlemen!"

"You fear my strength, Enkidu!"

"You fear my skill. You with your pathetic old sword, your pitiful bow—"

"Is this the Enkidu I loved, mocking me so?"

"You were the first to mock, when you threw back the shotgun into my hands, spurning my gift, calling me a coward—"

"The weapon, I said, was cowardly. Not you, Enkidu."

"It was the same thing."

"Bitte, bitte," said Schweitzer. "This is not the way!"

And again from Hemingway: "Gentlemen, please!"

They took no notice.

"I meant—"

"You said—"

"Shame—"

"Fear—"

"Three times over a coward!"

"Five times five a traitor!"

"False friend!"

"Vain braggart!"

"Gentlemen, I have to ask you—"

But Hemingway's voice, loud and firm though it was, was altogether drowned out by the roar of rage that came from the throat of Gilgamesh. Dizzying throbs of anger pounded in his breast, his throat, his temples. He could take no more. This was how it had begun the first time, when Enkidu had come to him with that shotgun and he had given it back and they had fallen into dispute. At first merely a disagreement, and then a hot debate, and then a quarrel, and then the hurling of bitter accusations. And then such words of anger as had never passed between them before, they who had been closer than brothers.

That time they hadn't come to blows. Enkidu had simply stalked away, declaring that their friendship was at an end. But now—hearing all the same words again, stymied by this quarrel even over the very method by which they were to fight—Gilgamesh could no longer restrain himself. Overmastered by fury and frustration, he rushed forward.

Enkidu, eyes gleaming, was ready for him.

Hemingway attempted to come between them. Big as he was, he was like a child next to Gilgamesh and Enkidu, and they swatted him to one side without effort. With a jolt that made the ground itself reverberate, Gilgamesh went crashing into Enkidu and laid hold of him with both hands.

Enkidu laughed. "So you have your way after all, King Gilgamesh! Bare hands it is!"

"It is the only way," said Gilgamesh.

At last. At last. There was no wrestler in this world or the other who could contend with Gilgamesh of Uruk. I will break him, Gilgamesh thought, as he broke our friendship. I will snap his spine. I will crush his chest.

As once they had done long ago, they fought like maddened bulls. They stared eye to eye as they contended. They grunted; they bellowed, they roared. Gilgamesh shouted out defiance in the language of Uruk and in any other language he could think of; and Enkidu muttered and stormed at Gilgamesh in the language of the beasts that once he had spoken when he was a wild man, the harsh growling of the lion of the plains.

Gilgamesh yearned to have Enkidu's life. He loved this man more dearly than life itself, and yet he prayed that it would be given him to break Enkidu's back, to hear the sharp snapping sound of his spine, to toss him aside like a worn-out cloak. So strong was his love that it had turned to the brightest of hatreds. I will send him to the Undertaker once again, Gilgamesh thought. I will hurl him from Hell.

But though he struggled as he had never struggled in combat before, Gilgamesh was unable to budge Enkidu. Veins bulged in his forehead; the sutures that held his wound burst and blood flowed down his arm; and still he strained to throw Enkidu to the ground, and still Enkidu held his place. And matched him, strength for strength, and kept him at bay. They stood locked that way a long moment, staring into each other's eyes, locked in unbreakable stalemate.

Then after a long while Enkidu said, as once he had said long ago, "Ah, Gilgamesh! There is not another one like you in all the world! Glory to the mother who bore you!"

It was like the breaking of a dam, and a rush of life-giving waters tumbling out over the summer-parched fields of the Land.

And from Gilgamesh in that moment of release and relief came twice-spoken words also:

"There is one other who is like me. But only one."

"No, for Enlil has given you the kingship."

"But you are my brother," said Gilgamesh, and they laughed and let go of each other and stepped back, as if seeing each other for the first time, and laughed again.

"This is great foolishness, this fighting between us," Enkidu cried.

"Very great foolishness indeed, brother."

"What need have you of shotguns and disruptors?"

"And what do I care if you choose to play with such toys?"

"Indeed, brother."

"Indeed!"

Gilgamesh looked away. They were all staring—the four party men, Lovecraft, Howard, the Hairy Man, Kublai Khan, Hemingway—all astonished, mouths drooping open. Only Schweitzer was beaming. The doctor came up to them and said quietly, "You have not injured each other? No. Gut. Gut. Then leave here, the two of you, together. Now. What do you care for Prester John and his wars, or for Mao and his? This is no business of yours. Go. Now."

Enkidu grinned. "What do you say, brother? Shall we go off hunting together?"

"To the end of the Outback, and back again. You and I, and no one else."

"And we will hunt only with our bows and spears?"

Gilgamesh shrugged. "With disruptors, if that is how you would have it. With cannons. With nuke grenades. Ah, Enkidu, Enkidu—!"

"Gilgamesh!"

"Go," Schweitzer whispered. "Now. Leave this place and never look back. Auf Wiedersehen! Gluckliche Reise! Gottes Name, go now!"

* * * *

Watching them take their leave, seeing them trudge off together into the swirling winds of the Outback, Robert Howard felt a sudden sharp pang of regret and loss. How beautiful they had been, those two heroes, those two giants, as they strained and struggled! And then that sudden magic moment when the folly of their quarrel came home to them, when they were enemies no longer and brothers once more—

And now they were gone, and here he stood amidst these others, these strangers—

He had wanted to be Gilgamesh's brother, or perhaps—he barely comprehended it—something more than a brother. But that could never have been. And, knowing that it could never have been, knowing that that man who seemed so much like his Conan was lost to him forever, Howard felt tears beginning to surge within him.

"Bob?" Lovecraft said. "Bob, are you all right?"

She-it, Howard thought. A man don't cry. Especially in front of other men.

He turned away, into the wind, so Lovecraft could not see his face.

"Bob? Bob?"

She-it, Howard thought again. And he let the tears come.

SUNDANCE

Today you liquidated about 50,000 Eaters in Sector A, and now you are spending an uneasy night. You and Herndon flew east at dawn, with the green-gold sunrise at your backs, and sprayed the neural pellets over a thousand hectares along the Forked River. You flew on into the prairie beyond the river, where the Eaters have already been wiped out, and had lunch sprawled on that thick, soft carpet of grass where the first settlement is expected to rise. Herndon picked some juiceflowers, and you enjoyed half an hour of mild hallucinations. Then, as you headed toward the copter to begin an afternoon of further pellet spraying, he said suddenly, “Tom, how would you feel about this if it turned out that the Eaters weren’t just animal pests? That they were people, say, with a language and rites and a history and all?”

You thought of how it had been for your own people.

“They aren’t,” you said.

“Suppose they were. Suppose the Eaters—”

"They aren't. Drop it."

Herndon has this streak of cruelty in him that leads him to ask such questions. He goes for the vulnerabilities; it amuses him. All night now his casual remark has echoed in your mind. Suppose the Eaters...suppose the Eaters...suppose...suppose...

You sleep for a while, and dream, and in your dreams you swim through rivers of blood.

Foolishness. A feverish fantasy. You know how important it is to exterminate the Eaters fast, before the settlers get here. They're just animals, and not even harmless animals at that; ecology-wreckers is what they are, devourers of oxygen-liberating plants, and they have to go. A few have been saved for zoological study. The rest must be destroyed. Ritual extirpation of undesirable beings, the old, old story. But let's not complicate our job with moral qualms, you tell yourself. Let's not dream of rivers of blood.

The Eaters don't even have blood, none that could flow in rivers, anyway. What they have is, well, a kind of lymph that permeates every tissue and transmits nourishment along the interfaces. Waste products go out the same way, osmotically. In terms of process, it's structurally analogous to your own kind of circulatory system, except there's no network of blood vessels hooked to a master pump. The life-stuff just oozes through their bodies as though they were amoebas or sponges or some other low-phylum form. Yet they're definitely high-phylum in nervous system, digestive setup, limb-and-organ template, etc. Odd, you think. The thing about aliens is that they're alien, you tell yourself, not for the first time.

The beauty of their biology for you and your companions is that it lets you exterminate them so neatly.

You fly over the grazing grounds and drop the neural pellets. The Eaters find and ingest them. Within an hour the poison has reached all sectors of the body. Life ceases; a rapid breakdown of cellular matter follows, the Eater literally falling apart molecule by molecule the instant that nutrition is cut off; the lymph-like stuff works like acid; a universal lysis occurs; flesh and even the bones, which are cartilaginous, dissolve. In two hours, a puddle on the ground. In four, nothing at all left. Considering how many millions of Eaters you've scheduled for extermination here, it's sweet of the bodies to be self-disposing. Otherwise what a charnel house this world would become!

Suppose the Eaters...

Damn Herndon. You almost feel like getting a memory-editing in the morning. Scrape his stupid speculations out of your head. If you dared. If you dared.

* * * *

In the morning he does not dare. Memory-editing frightens him; he will try to shake free of his newfound guilt without it. The Eaters, he explains to himself, are mindless herbivores, the unfortunate victims of human expansionism, but not really deserving of passionate defense. Their extermination is not tragic; it's just too bad. If Earthmen are to have this world, the Eaters must relinquish it. There's a difference, he tells himself, between the elimination of the Plains Indians from the American prairie in the nineteenth century and the destruction of the bison on that same prairie. One feels a little wistful about the slaughter of the thundering herds; one regrets the butchering of millions of the noble brown woolly beasts, yes. But one feels outrage, not mere wistful regret, at what was done to the Sioux. There's a difference. Reserve your passions for the proper cause.

He walks from his bubble at the edge of the camp toward the center of things. The flagstone path is moist and glistening. The morning fog has not yet lifted, and every tree is bowed, the long, notched leaves heavy with droplets of water. He pauses, crouching, to observe a spider-analog spinning its asymmetrical web. As he watches, a small amphibian, delicately shaded turquoise, glides as inconspicuously as possible over the mossy ground. Not inconspicuously enough; he gently lifts the little creature and puts it on the back of his hand. The gills flutter in anguish, and the amphibian's sides quiver. Slowly, cunningly, its color changes until it matches the coppery tone of the hand. The camouflage is excellent. He lowers his hand and the amphibian scurries into a puddle. He walks on.

He is forty years old, shorter than most of the other members of the expedition, with wide shoulders, a heavy chest, dark glossy hair, a blunt, spreading nose. He is a biologist. This is his third career, for he has failed as an anthropologist and as a developer of real estate. His name is Tom Two Ribbons. He has been married twice but has had no children. His great-grandfather died of alcoholism; his grandfather was addicted to hallucinogens; his father had compulsively visited cheap memory-editing parlors. Tom Two Ribbons is conscious that he is failing a family tradition, but he has not found his own mode of self-destruction.

In the main building he discovers Herndon, Julia, Ellen, Schwartz, Chang, Michaelson, and Nichols. They are eating breakfast; the others are already at work. Ellen rises and comes to him and kisses him. Her short soft yellow hair tickles his cheeks. "I love you," she whispers. She has spent the night in Michaelson's bubble. "I love you," he tells her, and draws a quick vertical line of affection between her small pale breasts. He winks at Michaelson, who nods, touches the tops of two fingers to his lips, and blows them a kiss. We are all good friends here, Tom Two Ribbons thinks.

"Who drops pellets today?" he asks.

"Mike and Chang," says Julia. "Sector C."

Schwartz says, "Eleven more days and we ought to have the whole peninsula clear. Then we can move inland."

"If our pellet supply holds up," Chang points out.

Herndon says, "Did you sleep well, Tom?"

"No," says Tom. He sits down and taps out his breakfast requisition. In the west, the fog is beginning to burn off the mountains. Something throbs in the back of his neck. He has been on this world nine weeks now, and in that time it has undergone its only change of season, shading from dry weather to foggy. The mists will remain for many months. Before the plains parch again, the Eaters will be gone and the settlers will begin to arrive. His food slides down the chute and he seizes it. Ellen sits beside him. She is a little more than half his age; this is her first voyage; she is their keeper of records, but she is also skilled at editing. “You look troubled,” Ellen tells him. “Can I help you?”

“No. Thank you.”

“I hate it when you get gloomy.”

“It’s a racial trait,” says Tom Two Ribbons.

“I doubt that very much.”

“The truth is that maybe my personality reconstruct is wearing thin. The trauma level was so close to the surface. I’m just a walking veneer, you know.”

Ellen laughs prettily. She wears only a sprayon half-wrap. Her skin looks damp; she and Michaelson have had a swim at dawn. Tom Two Ribbons is thinking of asking her to marry him, when this job is over. He has not been married since the collapse of the real estate business. The therapist suggested divorce as part of the reconstruct. He sometimes wonders where Terry has gone and whom she lives with now. Ellen says, “You seem pretty stable to me, Tom.”

“Thank you,” he says. She is young. She does not know.

"If it's just a passing gloom I can edit it out in one quick snip."

"Thank you," he says. "No."

"I forgot. You don't like editing."

"My father—"

"Yes?"

"In fifty years he pared himself down to a thread," Tom Two Ribbons says. "He had his ancestors edited away, his whole heritage, his religion, his wife, his sons, finally his name. Then he sat and smiled all day. Thank you, no editing."

"Where are you working today?" Ellen asks.

"In the compound, running tests."

"Want company? I'm off all morning."

"Thank you, no," he says, too quickly. She looks hurt. He tries to remedy his unintended cruelty by touching her arm lightly and saying, "Maybe this afternoon, all right? I need to commune a while. Yes?"

"Yes," she says, and smiles, and shapes a kiss with her lips.

After breakfast he goes to the compound. It covers a thousand hectares east of the base; they have bordered it with neutral-field projectors at intervals of eighty meters, and this is a sufficient fence to keep the captive population of two hundred Eaters from straying. When all the others have been exterminated, this study group will remain. At the southwest corner of the compound stands a lab bubble from which the experiments are run: metabolic, psychological, physiological, ecological. A stream crosses the compound diagonally. There is a low ridge of grassy hills at its eastern edge. Five distinct copses of tightly clustered knifeblade trees are separated by patches of dense savanna. Sheltered beneath the glass are the oxygen-plants, almost completely hidden except for the photosynthetic spikes that jut to heights of three or four meters at regular intervals, and the lemon-colored respiratory bodies, chest high, that make the grassland sweet and dizzying with exhaled gases. Through the fields move the Eaters in a straggling herd, nibbling delicately at the respiratory bodies.

Tom Two Ribbons spies the herd beside the stream and goes toward it. He stumbles over an oxygen-plant hidden in the grass but deftly recovers his balance and, seizing the puckered orifice of the respiratory body, inhales deeply. His despair lifts. He approaches the Eaters. They are spherical, bulky, slow-moving creatures, covered by masses of coarse orange fur. Saucer-like eyes protrude above narrow rubbery lips. Their legs are thin and scaly, like a chicken's, and their arms are short and held close to their bodies. They regard him with bland lack of curiosity. "Good morning, brothers!" is the way he greets them this time, and he wonders why.

* * * *

I noticed something strange today. Perhaps I simply sniffed too much oxygen in the fields; maybe I was succumbing to a suggestion Herndon planted; or possibly it's the family masochism cropping out. But while I was observing the Eaters in the compound, it seemed to me, for the first time, that they were behaving intelligently, that they were functioning in a ritualized way.

I followed them around for three hours. During that time they uncovered half a dozen outcroppings of oxygen-plants. In each case they went through a stylized pattern of action before starting to munch. They:

Formed a straggly circle around the plants.

Looked toward the sun.

Looked toward their neighbors on left and right around the circle.

Made fuzzy neighing sounds only after having done the foregoing.

Looked toward the sun again.

Moved in and ate.

If this wasn't a prayer of thanksgiving, a saying of grace, then what was it? And if they're advanced enough spiritually to say grace, are we not therefore committing genocide here? Do chimpanzees say grace? Christ, we wouldn't even wipe out chimps the way we're cleaning out the Eaters! Of course, chimps don't interfere with human crops, and some kind of coexistence would be possible, whereas Eaters and human agriculturalists simply can't function on the same planet. Nevertheless, there's a moral issue here. The liquidation effort is predicated on the assumption that the intelligence level of the Eaters is about on par with that of oysters, or, at best, sheep. Our consciences stay clear because our poison is quick and painless and because the Eaters thoughtfully dissolve upon dying, sparing us the mess of incinerating millions of corpses. But if they pray—

I won't say anything to the others just yet. I want more evidence, hard, objective. Films, tapes, record cubes. Then we'll see. What if I can show that we're exterminating intelligent beings? My family knows a little about genocide, after all, having been on the receiving end just a few centuries back. I doubt that I could halt what's going on here. But at the very least I could withdraw from the operation. Head back to Earth and stir up public outcries.

I hope I'm imagining this.

* * * *

I'm not imagining a thing. They gather in circles; they look to the sun; they neigh and pray. They're only balls of jelly on chicken-legs, but they give thanks for their food. Those big round eyes now seem to stare accusingly at me. Our tame herd here knows what's going on: that we have descended from the stars to eradicate their kind, and that they alone will be spared. They have no way of fighting back or even of communicating their displeasure, but they know. And hate us. Jesus, we have killed two million of them since we got here, and in a metaphorical sense I'm stained with blood, and what will I do, what can I do?

I must move very carefully, or I'll end up drugged and edited.

I can't let myself seem like a crank, a quack, an agitator. I can't stand up and denounce! I have to find allies. Herndon, first. He surely is onto the truth; he's the one who nudged me to it, that day we dropped pellets. And I thought he was merely being vicious in his usual way!

I'll talk to him tonight.

* * * *

He says, "I've been thinking about that suggestion you made. About the Eaters. Perhaps we haven't made sufficiently close psychological studies. I mean, if they really are intelligent—"

Herndon blinks. He is a tall man with glossy dark hair, a heavy beard, sharp cheekbones. "Who says they are, Tom?"

"You did. On the far side of the Forked River, you said—"

"It was just a speculative hypothesis. To make conversation."

"No, I think it was more than that. You really believed it."

Herndon looks troubled. "Tom, I don't know what you're trying to start, but don't start it. If I for a moment believed we were killing intelligent creatures, I'd run for an editor so fast I'd start an implosion wave."

"Why did you ask me that thing, then?" Tom Two Ribbons says.

"Idle chatter."

"Amusing yourself by kindling guilts in somebody else? You're a bastard, Herndon. I mean it."

"Well, look, Tom, if I had any idea that you'd get so worked up about a hypothetical suggestion—" Herndon shakes his head. "The Eaters aren't intelligent beings. Obviously. Otherwise we wouldn't be under orders to liquidate them."

"Obviously," says Tom Two Ribbons.

* * * *

Ellen said, "No, I don't know what Tom's up to. But I'm pretty sure he needs a rest. It's only a year and a half since his personality reconstruct, and he had a pretty bad breakdown back then."

Michaelson consulted a chart. "He's refused three times in a row to make his pellet-dropping run. Claiming he can't take time away from his research. Hell, we can fill in for him, but it's the idea that he's ducking chores that bothers me."

"What kind of research is he doing?" Nichols wanted to know.

"Not biological," said Julia. "He's with the Eaters in the compound all the time, but I don't see him making any tests on them. He just watches them."

"And talks to them," Chang observed.

"And talks, yes," Julia said.

"About what?" Nichols asked.

"Who knows?"

Everyone looked at Ellen. "You're closest to him," Michaelson said. "Can't you bring him out of it?"

"I've got to know what he's in, first," Ellen said. "He isn't saying a thing."

* * * *

You know that you must be very careful, for they outnumber you, and their concern for your welfare can be deadly. Already they realize you are disturbed, and Ellen has begun to probe for the source of the disturbance. Last night you lay in her arms and she questioned you, obliquely, skillfully, and you knew what she is trying to find out. When the moons appeared she suggested that you and she stroll in the compound, among the sleeping Eaters. You declined, but she sees that you have become involved with the creatures.

You have done probing of your own—subtly, you hope. And you are aware that you can do nothing to save the Eaters. An irrevocable commitment has been made. It is 1876 all over again; these are the bison, these are the Sioux, and they must be destroyed, for the railroad is on its way. If you speak out here, your friends will calm you and pacify you and edit you, for they do not see what you see. If you return to Earth to agitate, you will be mocked and recommended for another reconstruct. You can do nothing. You can do nothing.

You cannot save, but perhaps you can record.

Go out into the prairie. Live with the Eaters; make yourself their friend; learn their ways. Set it down, a full account of their culture, so that at least that much will not be lost. You know the techniques of field anthropology. As was done for your people in the old days, do now for the Eaters.

* * * *

He finds Michaelson. “Can you spare me for a few weeks?” he asks.

“Spare you, Tom? What do you mean?”

“I’ve got some field studies to do. I’d like to leave the base and work with Eaters in the wild.”

“What’s wrong with the ones in the compound?”

“It’s the last chance with wild ones, Mike. I’ve got to go.”

“Alone, or with Ellen?”

“Alone.”

Michaelson nods slowly. “All right, Tom. Whatever you want. Go. I won’t hold you here.”

* * * *

I dance in the prairie under the green-gold sun. About me the Eaters gather. I am stripped; sweat makes my skin glisten; my heart pounds. I talk to them with my feet, and they understand.

They understand.

They have a language of soft sounds. They have a god. They know love and awe and rapture. They have rites. They have names. They have a history. Of all this I am convinced.

I dance on thick grass.

How can I reach them? With my feet, with my hands, with my grunts, with my sweat. They gather by the hundreds, by the thousands, and I dance. I must not stop. They cluster about me and make their sounds. I am a conduit for strange forces. My great-grandfather should see me now! Sitting on his porch in Wyoming, the firewater in his hand, his brain rotting—see me now, old one! See the dance of Tom Two Ribbons! I talk to these strange ones with my feet under a sun that is the wrong color. I dance. I dance.

"Listen to me," I say. "I am your friend, I alone, the only one you can trust. Trust me, talk to me, teach me. Let me preserve your ways, for soon the destruction will come."

I dance, and the sun climbs, and the Eaters murmur.

There is the chief. I dance toward him, back, toward, I bow, I point to the sun, I imagine the being that lives in that ball of flame, I imitate the sounds of these people, I kneel, I rise, I dance. Tom Two Ribbons dances for you.

I summon skills my ancestors forgot. I feel the power flowing in me. As they danced in the days of the bison, I dance now, beyond the Forked River.

I dance, and now the Eaters dance too. Slowly, uncertainly, they move toward me, they shift their weight, lift leg and leg, sway about. "Yes, like that!" I cry. "Dance!"

We dance together as the sun reaches noon height.

Now their eyes are no longer accusing. I see warmth and kinship. I am their brother, their redskinned tribesman, he who dances with them. No longer do they seem clumsy to me. There is a strange ponderous grace in their movements. They dance. They dance. They caper about me. Closer, closer, closer!

We move in holy frenzy.

They sing, now, a blurred hymn of joy. They throw forth their arms, unclench their little claws. In unison they shift weight, left foot forward, right, left, right. Dance, brothers, dance, dance, dance! They press against me. Their flesh quivers; their smell is a sweet one. They gently thrust me across the field, to a part of the meadow where the grass is deep and untrampled. Still dancing, we seek for the oxygen-plants, and find clumps of them beneath the grass, and they make their prayer and seize them with their awkward arms, separating the respiratory bodies from the photosynthetic spikes. The plants, in anguish, release floods of oxygen. My mind reels. I laugh and sing. The Eaters are nibbling the lemon-colored perforated globes, nibbling the stalks as well. They thrust their plants at me. It is a religious ceremony, I see. Take from us, eat with us, join with us, this is the body, this is the blood, take, eat, join. I bend forward and put a lemon-colored globe to my lips. I do not bite; I nibble, as they do, my teeth slicing away the skin of the globe. Juice spurts into my mouth while oxygen drenches my nostrils. The Eaters sing hosannas. I should be in full paint for this, paint of my forefathers, feathers too, meeting their religion in the regalia of what should have been mine. Take, eat, join. The juice of the oxygen-plant flows in my veins. I embrace my brothers. I sing, and as my voice leaves my lips it becomes an arch that glistens like new steel, and I pitch my song lower, and the arch turns to tarnished silver. The Eaters crowd close. The scent of their bodies is fiery red to me. Their soft cries are puffs of steam. The sun is very warm; its rays are tiny jagged pings of puckered sound, close to the top of my range of hearing, plink! plink! plink! The thick grass hums to me, deep and rich, and the wind hurls points of flame along the prairie. I devour another oxygen-plant, and then a third. My brothers laugh and shout. They tell me of their gods, the god of warmth, the god of food, the god of pleasure, the god of death, the god of holiness, the god of wrongness, and the others. They recite for me the names of their kings, and I hear their voices as splashes of green mold on the clean sheet of the sky. They instruct me in their holy rites. I must remember this, I tell myself, for when it is gone it will never come again. I continue to dance. They continue to dance. The color of the hills becomes rough and coarse, like abrasive gas. Take, eat, join. Dance. They are so gentle!

I hear the drone of the copter, suddenly.

It hovers far overhead. I am unable to see who flies in it. "No!" I scream. "Not here! Not these people! Listen to me! This is Tom Ribbons! Can't you hear me? I'm doing a field study here! You've no right—!"

My voice makes spirals of blue moss edged with red sparks. They drift upward and are scattered by the breeze.

I yell, I shout, I bellow. I dance and shake my fists. From the wings of the copter the jointed arms of the pellet-distributors unfold. The gleaming spigots extend and whirl. The neural pellets rain down into the meadow, each tracing a blazing track that lingers in the sky. The sound of the copter becomes a furry carpet stretching to the horizon, and my shrill voice is lost in it.

The Eaters drift away from me, seeking the pellets, scratching at the roots of the grass to find them. Still dancing, I leap into their midst, striking the pellets from their hands, hurling them into the stream, crushing them to powder. The Eaters growl black needles at me. They turn away and search for more pellets. The copter turns and flies off, leaving a trail of dense oily sound. My brothers are gobbling the pellets eagerly.

There is no way to prevent it.

Joy consumes them and they topple and lie still. Occasionally a limb twitches; then even this stops. They begin to dissolve. Thousands of them melt on the prairie, sinking into shapelessness, losing spherical forms, flattening, ebbing into the ground. The bonds of the molecules will no longer hold. It is the twilight of protoplasm. They perish. They vanish. For hours I walk the prairie. Now I inhale oxygen; now I eat a lemon-colored globe. Sunset begins with the ringing of leaden chimes. Black clouds make brazen trumpet calls in the east and the deepening wind is a swirl of coaly bristles. Silence comes. Night falls. I dance. I am alone.

* * * *

The copter comes again, and they find you, and you do not resist as they gather you in. You are beyond bitterness. Quietly you explain what you have done and what you have learned, and why it is wrong to exterminate these people. You describe the plant you have eaten and the way it affects your senses, and as you talk of the blessed synesthesia, the texture of the wind and the sound of the clouds and the timbre of the sunlight, they nod and smile and tell you not to worry, that everything will be all right soon, and they touch something cold to your forearm, so cold that it is a whir and a buzz and the deintoxicant sinks into your vein and soon the ecstasy drains away, leaving only the exhaustion and the grief.

* * * *

He says, “We never learn a thing, do we? We export all our horrors to the stars. Wipe out the Armenians, wipe out the Jews, wipe out the Tasmanians, wipe out the Indians, wipe out everyone who’s in our way, and do the same damned murderous thing. You weren’t with me out there. You didn’t dance with them. You didn’t see what a rich, complex culture the Eaters have. Let me tell you about their tribal structure. It’s dense: seven levels of matrimonial relationships, to begin with, and an exogamy factor that requires—”

Softly Ellen says, “Tom, darling, nobody’s going to harm the Eaters.”

“And the religion,” he goes on. “Nine gods, each one an aspect of the god. Holiness and wrongness both worshiped. They have hymns, prayers, a theology. And we, the emissaries of the god of wrongness—”

"We're not exterminating them," Michaelson says. "Won't you understand that, Tom? This is all a fantasy of yours. You've been under the influence of drugs, but now we're clearing you out. You'll be clean in a little while. You'll have perspective again."

"A fantasy?" he says bitterly. "A drug dream? I stood out in the prairie and saw you drop pellets. And I watched them die and melt away. I didn't dream that."

"How can we convince you?" Chang asks earnestly. "What will make you believe? Shall we fly over the Eater country with you and show you how many millions there are?"

"But how many millions have been destroyed?" he demands.

They insist that he is wrong. Ellen tells him again that no one has ever desired to harm the Eaters. "This is a scientific expedition, Tom. We're here to study them. It's a violation of all we stand for to injure intelligent lifeforms."

"You admit that they're intelligent?"

"Of course. That's never been in doubt."

"Then why drop the pellets?" he asks. "Why slaughter them?"

"None of that has happened, Tom," Ellen says. She takes his hand between her cool palms. "Believe us. Believe us."

He says bitterly, "If you want me to believe you, why don't you do the job properly? Get out the editing machine and go to work on me. You can't simply talk me into rejecting the evidence of my own eyes."

"You were under drugs all the time," Michaelson says.

"I've never taken drugs! Except for what I ate in the meadow, when I danced—and that came after I had watched the massacre going on for weeks and weeks. Are you saying that it's a retroactive delusion?"

"No, Tom," Schwartz says. "You've had this delusion all along. It's part of your therapy, your reconstruct. You came here programmed with it."

"Impossible," he says.

Ellen kisses his fevered forehead. "It was done to reconcile you to mankind, you see. You had this terrible resentment of the displacement of your people in the nineteenth century. You were unable to forgive the industrial society for scattering the Sioux, and you were terribly full of hate. Your therapist thought that if you could be made to participate in an imaginary modern extermination, if you could come to see it as a necessary operation, you'd be purged of your resentment and able to take your place in society as—"

He thrusts her away. "Don't talk idiocy! If you knew the first thing about reconstruct therapy, you'd realize that no reputable therapist could be so shallow. There are no one-to-one correlations in reconstructs. No, don't touch me. Keep away. Keep away."

He will not let them persuade him that this is merely a drug-born dream. It is no fantasy, he tells himself, and it is no therapy. He rises. He goes out. They do not follow him. He takes a copter and seeks his brothers.

* * * *

The sun is much hotter today. The Eaters are more numerous. Today I wear paint, today I wear feathers. My body shines with my sweat. They dance with me, and they have a frenzy in them that I have never seen before. We pound the trampled meadow with our feet. We clutch for the sun with our hands. We sing, we shout, we cry. We will dance until we fall.

This is no fantasy. These people are real, and they are intelligent, and they are doomed. This I know.

We dance. Despite the doom, we dance.

My great-grandfather comes and dances with us. He too is real. His nose is like a hawk's, not blunt like mine, and he wears the big headdress, and his muscles are like cords under his brown skin. He sings, he shouts, he cries.

Others of my family join us.

We eat the oxygen-plants together. We embrace the Eaters. We know, all of us, what it is to be hunted.

The clouds make music and the wind takes on texture and the sun's warmth has color.

We dance. We dance. Our limbs know no weariness.

The sun grows and fills the whole sky, and I see no Eaters now, only my own people, my father's fathers across the centuries, thousands of gleaming skins, thousands of hawk's noses, and we eat the plants, and we find sharp sticks and thrust them into our flesh, and the sweet blood flows and dries in the blaze of the sun, and we dance, and we dance, and some of us fall from weariness, and we dance, and the prairie is a sea of bobbing headdresses, an ocean of feathers, and we dance, and my heart makes thunder, and my knees become water, and the sun's fire engulfs me, and I dance, and I fall, and I dance, and I fall, and I fall, and I fall.

* * * *

Again they find you and bring you back. They give you the cool snout on your arm to take the oxygen-plant drug from your veins, and then they give you something else so you will rest. You rest and you are very calm. Ellen kisses you and you stroke her soft skin, and then the others come in and they talk to you, saying soothing things, but you do not listen, for you are searching for realities. It is not an easy search. It is like falling through many trapdoors, looking for the one room whose floor is not hinged. Everything that has happened on this planet is your therapy, you tell yourself, designed to reconcile an embittered aborigine to the white man's conquest; nothing is really being exterminated here. You reject that and fall through and realize that this must be the therapy of your friends; they carry the weight of accumulated centuries of guilts and have come here to shed that load, and you are here to ease them of their burden, to draw their sins into yourself and give them forgiveness. Again you fall through, and see that the Eaters are mere animals who threaten the ecology and must be removed; the culture you imagined for them is your hallucination, kindled out of old churnings. You try to withdraw your objections to this necessary extermination, but you fall through again and discover that there is no extermination except in your mind, which is troubled and disordered by your obsession with the crime against your ancestors, and you sit up, for you wish to apologize to these friends of yours, these innocent scientists whom you have called murderers. And you fall through.

IN ENTROPY'S JAWS

Static crackles from the hazy golden cloud of airborne loudspeakers drifting just below the ceiling of the spaceliner cabin. A hiss: communications filters are opening. An impending announcement from the bridge, no doubt. Then the captain's bland, mechanical voice: "We are approaching the Panama Canal. All passengers into their bottles until the all-clear after insertion. When we come out the far side, we'll be travelling at eighty lights toward the Perseus relay booster. Thank you." In John Skein's cabin the warning globe begins to flash, dousing him with red, yellow, green light, going up and down the visible spectrum, giving him some infra– and ultra– too. Not everybody who books passage on this liner necessarily has human sensory equipment. The signal will not go out until Skein is safely in his bottle. Go on, it tells him. Get in. Get in. Panama Canal coming up.

Obediently he rises and moves across the narrow cabin toward the tapering dull-skinned steel container, two and a half meters high, that will protect him against the dimensional stresses of canal insertion. He is a tall, angular man with thin lips, a strong chin, glossy black hair that clings close to his high-vaulted skull. His skin is deeply tanned but his eyes are those of one who has been in winter for some time. This is the fiftieth year of his second go-round. He is travelling alone toward a world of the Abbondanza system, perhaps the last leg on a journey that has occupied him for several years.

The passenger bottle swings open on its gaudy rhodium-jacketed hinge when its sensors, picking up Skein's mass and thermal output, tell it that its protectee is within entry range. He gets in. It closes and seals, wrapping him in a seamless magnetic field. "Please be seated," the bottle tells him softly. "Place your arms through the stasis loops and your feet in the security platens. When you have done this the pressor fields will automatically be activated and you will be fully insulated against injury during the coming period of turbulence." Skein, who has had plenty of experience with faster-than-light travel, has anticipated the instructions and is already in stasis. The bottle closes. "Do you wish music?" it asks him. "A book? A vision spool? Conversation?"

"Nothing, thanks," Skein says, and waits.

He understands waiting very well by this time. Once he was an impatient man, but this is a thin season in his life, and it has been teaching him the arts of stoic acceptance. He will sit here with the Buddha's own complacency until the ship is through the canal. Silent, alone, self-sufficient. If only there will be no fugues this time. Or, at least—he is negotiating the terms of his torment with his demons—at least let them not be flashforwards. If he must break loose again from the matrix of time, he prefers to be cast only into his yesterdays, never into his tomorrows.

"We are almost into the canal now," the bottle tells him pleasantly.

"It's all right. You don't need to look after me. Just let me know when it's safe to come out."

He closes his eyes. Trying to envision the ship: a fragile glimmering purple needle squirting through clinging blackness, plunging toward the celestial vortex just ahead, the maelstrom of clashing forces, the soup of contravariant tensors. The Panama Canal, so-called. Through which the liner will shortly rush, acquiring during its passage such a garland of borrowed power that it will rip itself free of the standard fourspace; it will emerge on the far side of the canal into a strange, tranquil pocket of the universe where the speed of light is the downside limiting velocity, and no one knows where the upper limit lies.

Alarms sound in the corridor, heavy, resonant: clang, clang, clang. The dislocation is beginning. Skein is braced. What does it look like out there? Folds of glowing black velvet, furry swatches of the disrupted continuum, wrapping themselves around the ship? Titanic lightnings hammering on the hull? Laughing centaurs flashing across the twisted heavens? Despondent masks, fixed in tragic grimaces, dangling between the blurred stars? Streaks of orange, green, crimson: sick rainbows, limp, askew? In we go. Clang, clang, clang. The next phase of the voyage now begins. He thinks of his destination, holding an image of it rigidly in mind. The picture is vivid, though this is a world he has visited only in spells of temporal fugue. Too often; he has been there again and again in these moments of disorientation in time. The colors are wrong on that world. Purple sand. Blue-leaved trees. Too much manganese? Too little copper? He will forgive it its colors if it will grant him his answers. And then. Skein feels the familiar ugly throbbing at the base of his neck, as if the tip of his spine is swelling like a balloon. He curses. He tries to resist. As he feared, not even the bottle can wholly protect him against these stresses. Outside the ship the universe is being wrenched apart; some of that slips in here and throws him into a private epilepsy of the timeline. Spacetime is breaking up for him. He will go into fugue. He clings, fighting, knowing it is futile. The currents of time buffet him, knocking him a short distance into the future, then a reciprocal distance into the past, as if he is a bubble of insect spittle glued loosely to a dry reed. He cannot hold on much longer. Let it not be flashforward, he prays, wondering who it is to whom he prays. Let it not be flashforward. And he loses his grip. And shatters. And is swept in shards across time.

* * * *

Of course, if x is before y then it remains eternally before y, and nothing in the passage of time can change this. But the peculiar position of the "now" can be easily expressed simply because our language has tenses. The future will be, the present is, and the past was; the light will be red, it is now yellow, and it was green. But do we, in these terms, really describe the "processional" character of time? We sometimes say that an event is future, then it is present, and finally it is past; and by this means we seem to dispense with tenses, yet we portray the passage of time. But this is really not the case; for all that we have done is to translate our tenses into the words "then" and "finally", and into the order in which we state our clauses. If we were to omit these words or their equivalents, and mix up the clauses, our sentences would no longer be meaningful. To say that the future, the present, and the past are in some sense is to dodge the problem of time by resorting to the tenseless language of logic and mathematics. In such an atemporal language it would be meaningful to say that Socrates is mortal because all men are mortal and Socrates is a man, even though Socrates has been dead many centuries. But if we cannot describe time either by a language containing tenses or by a tenseless language, how shall we symbolize it?

* * * *

He feels the curious doubleness of self, the sense of having been here before, and knows it is flashback. Some comfort in that. He is a passenger in his own skull, looking out through the eyes of John Skein on an event that he has already experienced, and which he now is powerless to alter.

His office. All its gilded magnificence. A crystal dome at the summit of Kenyatta Tower. With the amplifiers on he can see as far as Serengeti in one direction, Mombasa in another. Count the fleas on an elephant in Tsavo Park. A wall of light on the east-southeast face of the dome, housing his data-access units. No one can stare at that wall more than thirty seconds without suffering intensely from a surfeit of information. Except Skein; he drains nourishment from it, hour after hour.

As he slides into the soul of that earlier Skein he takes a brief joy in the sight of his office, like Aeneas relishing a vision of unfallen Troy, like Adam looking back into Eden. How good it was. That broad sweet desk with its subtle components dedicated to his service. The gentle psychosensitive carpet, so useful and so beautiful. The undulating ribbon-sculpture gliding in and out of the dome's skin, undergoing molecular displacement each time and forever exhibiting the newest of its infinity of possible patterns. A rich man's office; he was unabashed in his pursuit of elegance. He had earned the right to luxury through the intelligent use of his innate skills. Returning now to that lost dome of wonders, he quickly seizes his moment of satisfaction, aware that shortly some souring scene of subtraction will be replayed for him, one of the stages of the darkening and withering of his life. But which one?

"Send in Coustakis," he hears himself say, and his words give him the answer. That one. He will again watch his own destruction. Surely there is no further need to subject him to this particular reenactment. He has been through it at least seven times; he is losing count. An endless spiralling track of torment.

Coustakis is bald, blue-eyed, sharp-nosed, with the desperate look of a man who is near the end of his first go-round and is not yet sure that he will be granted a second. Skein guesses that he is about seventy. The man is unlikable: he dresses coarsely, moves in aggressive blurting little strides, and shows in every gesture and glance that he seethes with envy of the opulence with which Skein surrounds himself. Skein feels no need to like his clients, though. Only to respect. And Coustakis is brilliant; he commands respect.

Skein says, "My staff and I have studied your proposal in great detail. It's a cunning scheme."

"You'll help me?"

"There are risks for me," Skein points out. "Nissenson has a powerful ego. So do you. I could get hurt. The whole concept of synergy involves risk for the Communicator. My fees are calculated accordingly."

"Nobody expects a Communicator to be cheap," Coustakis mutters.

"I'm not. But I think you'll be able to afford me. The question is whether I can afford you."

"You're very cryptic, Mr. Skein. Like all oracles."

Skein smiles. "I'm not an oracle, I'm afraid. Merely a conduit through whom connections are made. I can't foresee the future."

"You can evaluate probabilities."

"Only concerning my own welfare. And I'm capable of arriving at an incorrect evaluation."

Coustakis fidgets. "Will you help me or won't you?"

"The fee," Skein says, "is half a million down, plus an equity position of fifteen percent in the corporation you'll establish with the contacts I provide."

Coustakis gnaws at his lower lip. "So much?"

"Bear in mind that I've got to split my fee with Nissenson. Consultants like him aren't cheap."

"Even so. Ten percent."

"Excuse me, Mr. Coustakis. I really thought we were past the point of negotiation in this transaction. It's going to be a busy day for me, and so—" Skein passes his hand over a black rectangle on his desk and a section of the floor silently opens, uncovering the dropshaft access. He nods toward it. The carpet reveals the colors of Coustakis's mental processes: black for anger, green for greed, red for anxiety, yellow for fear, blue for temptation, all mixed together in the hashed pattern betraying the calculations now going on in his mind. Coustakis will yield. Nevertheless Skein proceeds with the charade of standing, gesturing toward the exit, trying to usher his visitor out. "All right," Coustakis says explosively, "fifteen percent!"

Skein instructs his desk to extrude a contract cube. He says, "Place your hand here, please," and as Coustakis touches the cube he presses his own palm against its opposite face. At once the cube's sleek crystalline surface darkens and roughens as the double sensory output bombards it. Skein says, "Repeat after me. I, Nicholas Coustakis, whose handprint and vibration pattern are being imprinted in this contract as I speak—"

"I, Nicholas Coustakis, whose handprint and vibration pattern are being imprinted in this contract as I speak—"

"—do knowingly and willingly assign to John Skein Enterprises, as payment for professional services to be rendered, an equity interest in Coustakis Transport Ltd or any successor corporation amounting to—"

"—do knowingly and willingly assign—"

They drone on in turns through a description of Coustakis's corporation and the irrevocable nature of Skein's part ownership in it. Then Skein files the contract cube and says, "If you'll phone your bank and put your thumb on the cash part of the transaction, I'll make contact with Nissenson and you can get started."

"Half a million?"

"Half a million."

"You know I don't have that kind of money."

"Let's not waste time, Mr. Coustakis. You have assets. Pledge them as collateral. Credit is easily obtained."

Scowling, Coustakis applies for the loan, gets it, transfers the funds to Skein's account. The process takes eight minutes; Skein uses the time to review Coustakis's ego profile. It displeases Skein to have to exert such sordid economic pressure; but the service he offers does, after all, expose him to dangers, and he must cushion the risk by high guarantees, in case some mishap should put him out of business.

"Now we can proceed," Skein says, when the transaction is done.

Coustakis has almost invented a system for the economical instantaneous transportation of matter. It will not, unfortunately, ever be useful for living things, since the process involves the destruction of the material being shipped and its virtually simultaneous reconstitution elsewhere. The fragile entity that is the soul cannot withstand the withering blast of Coustakis's transmitter's electron beam. But there is tremendous potential in the freight business; the Coustakis transmitter will be able to send cabbages to Mars, computers to Pluto, and, given the proper linkage facilities, it should be able to reach the inhabited extrasolar planets.

However, Coustakis has not yet perfected his system. For five years he has been stymied by one impassable problem: keeping the beam tight enough between transmitter and receiver. Beamspread has led to chaos in his experiments; marginal straying results in the loss of transmitted information, so that that which is being sent invariably arrives incomplete. Coustakis has depleted his resources in the unsuccessful search for a solution, and thus has been forced to the desperate and costly step of calling in a Communicator.

For a price, Skein will place him in contact with someone who can solve his problem. Skein has a network of consultants on several worlds, experts in technology and finance and philology and nearly everything else. Using his own mind as the focal nexus, Skein will open telepathic communion between Coustakis and a consultant.

"Get Nissenson into a receptive state," he orders his desk.

Coustakis, blinking rapidly, obviously uneasy, says, "First let me get it clear. This man will see everything that's in my mind? He'll get access to my secrets?"

"No. No. I filter the communion with great care. Nothing will pass from your mind to his except the nature of the problem you want him to tackle. Nothing will come back from his mind to yours except the answer."

"And if he doesn't have the answer?"

"He will."

Skein gives no refunds in the event of failure, but he has never had a failure. He does not accept jobs that he feels will be inherently impossible to handle. Either Nissenson will see the solution Coustakis has been overlooking, or else he will make some suggestion that will nudge Coustakis toward finding the solution himself. The telepathic communion is the vital element. Mere talking would never get anywhere. Coustakis and Nissenson could stare at blueprints together for months, pound computers side by side for years, debate the difficulty with each other for decades, and still they might not hit on the answer. But the communion creates a synergy of minds that is more than a doubling of the available brainpower. A union of perceptions, a heightening, that always produces that mystic flash of insight, that leap of the intellect.

"And if he goes into the transmission business for himself afterward?" Coustakis asks.

"He's bonded," Skein says curtly. "No chance of it. Let's go, now. Up and together."

The desk reports that Nissenson, half the world away in São Paulo, is ready. Skein's power does not vary with distance. Quickly he throws Coustakis into the receptive condition, and swings around to face the brilliant lights of his data-access units. Those sparkling, shifting little blazes kindle his gift, jabbing at the electrical rhythms of his brain until he is lifted into the energy level that permits the opening of a communion. As he starts to go up, the other

Skein who is watching, the time-displaced prisoner behind his forehead, tries frenziedly to prevent him from entering the fatal linkage. Don't. Don't. You'll overload. They're too strong for you. Easier to halt a planet in its orbit, though. The course of the past is frozen; all this has already happened; the Skein who cries out in silent anguish is merely an observer, necessarily passive, here to view the maiming of his earlier self.

Skein reaches forth one tendril of his mind and engages Nissenson. With another tendril he snares Coustakis. Steadily, now, he draws the two tendrils together.

There is no way to predict the intensity of the forces that will shortly course through his brain. He has done what he could, checking the ego profiles of his client and the consultant, but that really tells him little. What Coustakis and Nissenson may be as individuals hardly matters; it is what they may become in communion that he must fear. Synergistic intensities are unpredictable. He has lived for a lifetime and a half with the possibility of a burnout.

The tendrils meet.

Skein the observer winces and tries to armor himself against the shock. But there is no way to deflect it. Out of Coustakis's mind flows a description of the matter transmitter and a clear statement of the beam-spread problem; Skein shoves it along to Nissenson, who begins to work on a solution. But when their minds join it is immediately evident that their combined strength will be more than Skein can control. This time the synergy will destroy him. But he cannot disengage; he has no mental circuitbreaker. He is caught, trapped, impaled. The entity that is Coustakis/Nissenson will not let go of him, for that would mean its own destruction. A wave of mental energy goes rippling and dancing along the vector of communion from Coustakis to Nissenson and goes bouncing back, pulsating and gaining strength, from Nissenson to Coustakis. A fiery oscillation is set up. Skein sees what is happening; he has become the amplifier of his own doom. The torrent of energy continues to gather power each time it reverberates from Coustakis to Nissenson, from Nissenson to Coustakis. Powerless, Skein watches the energy-pumping effect building up a mighty charge. The discharge is bound to come soon, and he will be the one who must receive it. How long? How long? The juggernaut fills the corridors of his mind. He ceases to know which end of the circuit is Nissenson, which is Coustakis; he perceives only two shining walls of mental power, between which he is stretched ever thinner, a twanging wire of ego, heating up, heating up, glowing now, emitting a searing blast of heat, particles of identity streaming away from him like so many liberated ions—

Then he lies numb and dazed on the floor of his office, grinding his face into the psychosensitive carpet, while Coustakis barks over and over, "Skein? Skein? Skein? Skein?"

* * * *

Like any other chronometric device, our inner clocks are subject to their own peculiar disorders and, in spite of the substantial concordance between private and public time, discrepancies may occur as the result of sheer inattention. Mach noted that if a doctor focuses his attention on the patient's blood, it may seem to him to squirt out before the lancet enters the skin and, for similar reasons, the feebler of two stimuli presented simultaneously is usually perceived later...Normal life requires the capacity to recall experiences in a sequence corresponding, roughly at least, to the order in which they actually occurred. It requires in addition that our potential recollections should be reasonably accessible to consciousness. These potential recollections mean not only a perpetuation within us of representations of the past, but also a ceaseless interplay between such representations and the uninterrupted input of present information from the external world. Just as our past may be at the service of our present, so the present may be remotely controlled by our past: in the words of Shelley, "Swift as a Thought by the snake Memory stung."

* * * *

"Skein? Skein? Skein? Skein?"

His bottle is open and they are helping him out. His cabin is full of intruders. Skein recognizes the captain's robot, the medic, and a couple of passengers, the little swarthy man from Pingalore and the woman from Globe Fifteen. The cabin door is open and more people are coming in. The medic makes a cuff-shooting gesture and a blinding haze of metallic white particles wraps itself about Skein's head. The little tingling prickling sensations spur him to wakefulness. "You didn't respond when the bottle told you it was all right," the medic explains. "We're through the canal."

"Was it a good passage? Fine. Fine. I must have dozed."

"If you'd like to come to the infirmary—routine check, only—put you through the diagnostat—"

"No. No. Will you all please go? I assure you, I'm quite all right."

Reluctantly, clucking over him, they finally leave. Skein gulps cold water until his head is clear. He plants himself flatfooted in mid-cabin, trying to pick up some sensation of forward motion. The ship now is travelling at something like fifteen million miles a second. How long is fifteen million miles? How long is a second? From Rome to Naples it was a morning's drive on the autostrada. From Tel Aviv to Jerusalem was the time between twilight and darkness. San Francisco to San Diego spanned lunch to dinner by superpod. As I slide my right foot two inches forward we traverse fifteen million miles. From where to where? And why? He has not seen Earth in twenty-six months. At the end of this voyage his remaining funds will be exhausted. Perhaps he will have to make his home in the Abbondanza system; he has no return ticket. But of course he can travel to his heart's discontent within his own skull, whipping from point to point along the timeline in the grip of the fugues.

He goes quickly from his cabin to the recreation lounge.

The ship is a second-class vessel, neither lavish nor seedy. It carries about twenty passengers, most of them, like him, bound outward on one-way journeys. He has not talked directly to any of them, but he has done considerable eavesdropping in the lounge, and by now can tag each one of them with the proper dull biography. The wife bravely joining her pioneer husband, whom she has not seen for half a decade. The remittance man under orders to place ten thousand light-years, at the very least, between himself and his parents. The glittery-eyed entrepreneur, a Phoenician merchant sixty centuries after his proper era, off to carve an empire as a middleman's middleman. The tourists. The bureaucrat. The colonel. Among this collection Skein stands out in sharp relief; he is the only one who has not made an effort to know and be known, and the mystery of his reserve tantalizes them.

He carries the fact of his crackup with him like some wrinkled dangling yellowed wen. When his eyes meet those of any of the others he says silently, You see my deformity? I am my own survivor. I have been destroyed and lived to look back on it. Once I was a man of wealth and power, and look at me now. But I ask for no pity. Is that understood?

Hunching at the bar, Skein pushes the node for filtered rum. His drink arrives, and with it comes the remittance man, handsome, young, insinuating. Giving Skein a confidential wink, as if to say, I know. You're on the run, too.

"From Earth, are you?" he says to Skein.

"Formerly."

"I'm Pid Rocklin."

"John Skein."

"What were you doing there?"

"On Earth?" Skein shrugs. "A Communicator. I retired four years ago."

"Oh." Rocklin summons a drink. "That's good work, if you have the gift."

"I had the gift," Skein says. The unstressed past tense is as far into self-pity as he will go. He drinks and pushes for another one. A great gleaming screen over the bar shows the look of space: empty, here beyond the Panama Canal, although yesterday a million suns blazed on that ebony rectangle. Skein imagines he can hear the whoosh of hydrogen molecules scraping past the hull at eighty lights. He sees them as blobs of brightness millions of miles long, going zip! and zip! and zip! as the ship spurts along. Abruptly a purple nimbus envelopes him and he drops into a flashforward fugue so quickly there is not even time for the usual futile resistance. "Hey, what's the matter?" Pid Rocklin says, reaching for him. "Are you all—" and Skein loses the universe.

* * * *

He is on the world that he takes to be Abbondanza VI, and his familiar companion, the skull-faced man, stands beside him at the edge of an oily orange sea. They appear to be having the debate about time once again. The skull-faced man must be at least a hundred and twenty years old; his skin lies against his bones with, seemingly, no flesh at all under it, and his face is all nostrils and burning eyes. Bony sockets, sharp shelves for cheekbones, a bald dome of a skull. The neck no more than wrist-thick, rising out of shrivelled shoulders. Saying, "Won't you ever come to see that causality is merely an illusion, Skein? The notion that there's a consecutive series of events is nothing but a fraud. We impose form on our lives, we talk of time's arrow, we say that there's a flow from A through G and Q to Z, we make believe everything is nicely linear. But it isn't, Skein. It isn't."

"So you keep telling me."

"I feel an obligation to awaken your mind to the truth. G can come before A, and Z before both of them. Most of us don't like to perceive it that way, so we arrange things in what seems like a more logical pattern, just as a novelist will put the motive before the murder and the murder before the arrest. But the universe isn't a novel. We can't make nature imitate art. It's all random, Skein, random, random! Look there. You see what's drifting on the sea?"

On the orange waves tosses the bloated corpse of a shaggy blue beast. Upturned saucery eyes, drooping snout, thick limbs. Why is it not waterlogged by now? What keeps it afloat?

The skull-faced man says, "Time is an ocean, and events come drifting to us as randomly as dead animals on the waves. We filter them. We screen out what doesn't make sense and admit them to our consciousness in what seems to be the right sequence." He laughs. "The grand delusion! The past is nothing but a series of films slipping unpredictably into the future. And vice versa."

"I won't accept that," Skein says stubbornly. "It's a demonic, chaotic, nihilistic theory. It's idiocy. Are we greybeards before we're children? Do we die before we're born? Do trees devolve into seeds? Deny linearity all you like. I won't go along."

"You can say that after all you've experienced?"

Skein shakes his head. "I'll go on saying it. What I've been going through is a mental illness. Maybe I'm deranged, but the universe isn't."

"Contrary. You've only recently become sane and started to see things as they really are," the skull-faced man insists. "The trouble is that you don't want to admit the evidence you've begun to perceive. Your filters are down, Skein! You've shaken free of the illusion of linearity! Now's your chance to show your resilience. Learn to live with the real reality. Stop this silly business of imposing an artificial order on the flow of time. Why should effect follow cause? Why shouldn't the seed follow the tree? Why must you persist in holding tight to a useless, outworn, contemptible system of false evaluations of experience when you've managed to break free of the—"

"Stop it! Stop it! Stop it! Stop it!"

* * * *

"—right, Skein?"

"What happened?"

"You started to fall off your stool," Pid Rocklin says. "You turned absolutely white. I thought you were having some kind of a stroke."

"How long was I unconscious?"

"Oh, three, four seconds, I suppose. I grabbed you and propped you up, and your eyes opened. Can I help you to your cabin? Or maybe you ought to go to the infirmary."

"Excuse me," Skein says hoarsely, and leaves the lounge.

When the hallucinations began, not long after the Coustakis overload, he assumed at first that they were memory disturbances produced by the fearful jolt he had absorbed. Quite clearly most of them involved scenes of his past, which he would relive, during the moments of fugue, with an intensity so brilliant that he felt he had actually been thrust back into time. He did not merely recollect, but rather he experienced the past anew, following a script from which he could not deviate as he spoke and felt and reacted. Such strange excursions into memory could be easily enough explained: his brain had been damaged, and it was heaving old segments of experience into view in some kind of attempt to clear itself of debris and heal the wounds. But while the flashbacks were comprehensible, the flashforwards were not, and he did not recognize them at all for what they actually were. Those scenes of himself wandering alien worlds, those phantom conversations with people he had never met, those views of spaceliner cabins and transit booths and unfamiliar hotels and passenger terminals, seemed merely to be fantasies, random fictions of his injured brain. Even when he started to notice that there was a consistent pattern to these feverish glimpses of the unknown, he still did not catch on. It appeared as though he was seeing himself performing a sort of quest, or perhaps a pilgrimage; the slices of unexperienced experience that he was permitted to see began to fit into a coherent structure of travel and seeking. And certain scenes and conversations recurred, yes, sometimes several times the same day, the script always the same, so that he began to learn a few of the scenes word for word. Despite the solid texture of these episodes, he persisted in thinking of them as mere brief flickering segments of nightmare. He could not imagine why the injury to his brain was causing him to have these waking dreams of long space voyages and unknown planets, so vivid and so momentarily real, but they seemed no more frightening to him than the equally vivid flashbacks.

Only after a while, when many months had passed since the Coustakis incident, did the truth strike him. One day he found himself living through an episode that he considered to be one of his fantasies. It was a minor thing, one that he had experienced, in whole or in part, seven or eight times. What he had seen, in fitful bursts of uninvited delusion, was himself in a public garden on some hot spring morning, standing before an immense baroque building while a grotesque group of nonhuman tourists filed past him in a weird creaking, clanking procession of inhalator suits and breather-wheels and ion-disperser masks. That was all. Then it happened that a harrowing legal snarl brought him to a city in North Carolina about fourteen months after the overload, and, after having put in his appearance at the courthouse, he set out on a long walk through the grimy, decayed metropolis, and came, as if by an enchantment, to a huge metal gate behind which he could see a dark sweep of lavish forest, oaks and rhododendrons and magnolias, laid out in an elegant formal manner. It was, according to a sign posted by the gate, the estate of a nineteenth-century millionaire, now open to all and preserved in its ancient state despite the encroachments of the city on its borders.

Skein bought a ticket and went in, on foot, hiking for what seemed like miles through cool leafy glades, until abruptly the path curved and he emerged into the bright sunlight and saw before him the great grey bulk of a colossal mansion, hundreds of rooms topped by parapets and spires, with a massive portico from which vast columns of stairs descended. In wonder he moved toward it, for this was the building of his frequent fantasy, and as he approached he beheld the red and green and purple figures crossing the portico, those coiled and gnarled and looping shapes he had seen before, the eerie horde of alien travellers here to take in the wonders of Earth. Heads without eyes, eyes without heads, multiplicities of limbs and absences of limbs, bodies like tumors and tumors like bodies, all the universe's imagination on display in these agglomerated life forms, so strange and yet not at all strange to him. But this time it was no fantasy. It fit smoothly into the sequence of the events of the day, rather than dropping, dreamlike, intrusive, into that sequence. Nor did it fade after a few moments; the scene remained sharp, never leaving him to plunge back into "real" life. This was reality itself, and he had experienced it before.

Twice more in the next few weeks things like that happened to him, until at last he was ready to admit the truth to himself about his fugues, that he was experiencing flashforwards as well as flashbacks, that he was being subjected to glimpses of his own future.

* * * *

T'ang, the high king of the Shang, asked Hsia Chi saying, "In the beginning, were there already individual things?" Hsia Chi replied, "If there were no things then, how could there be any now? If later generations should pretend that there had been no things in our time, would they be right?" Tang said, "Have things then no before and no after?" To which Hsia Chi replied, "The ends and the origins of things have no limit from which they began. The origin of one thing may be considered the end of another; the end of one may be considered the origin of the next. Who can distinguish accurately between these cycles? What lies beyond all things, and before all events, we cannot know."

* * * *

They reach and enter the Perseus relay booster, which is a whirling celestial anomaly structurally similar to the Panama Canal but not nearly so potent, and it kicks the ship's velocity to just above a hundred lights. That is the voyage's final acceleration; the ship will maintain this rate for two and a half days, until it clocks in at Scylla, the main deceleration station for this part of the galaxy, where it will be seized by a spongy web of forces twenty light-minutes in diameter and slowed to sublight velocities for the entry into the Abbondanza system.

Skein spends nearly all of this period in his cabin, rarely eating and sleeping very little. He reads, almost constantly, obsessively dredging from the ship's extensive library a wide and capricious assortment of books. Rilke. Kafka. Eddington, The Nature of the Physical World. Lowry, Hear Us O Lord From Heaven Thy Dwelling Place. Elias. Razhuminin. Dickey. Pound. Fraisse, The Psychology of Time. Greene, Dream and Delusion. Poe. Shakespeare. Marlowe. Tourneur. The Waste Land. Ulysses. Heart of Darkness. Bury, The Idea of Progress. Jung. Buechner. Pirandello. The Magic Mountain. Ellis, The Rack. Cervantes. Blenheim. Fierst. Keats. Nietzsche. His mind swims with images and bits of verse, with floating sequences of dialogue, with unscaffolded dialectics. He dips into each work briefly, magpielike, seeking bright scraps. The words form a scaly impasto on the inner surface of his skull. He finds that this heavy verbal overdose helps, to some slight extent, to fight off the fugues;

his mind is weighted, perhaps, bound by this leaden clutter of borrowed genius to the moving line of the present, and during his debauch of reading he finds himself shifting off that line less frequently than in the recent past.

His mind whirls. Man is a rope stretched between the animal and the Superman—A rope over an abyss. My patience are exhausted. See, see where Christ's blood streams in the firmament! One drop would save my soul. I had not thought death had undone so many. These fragments I have shored against my ruins. Hoogspanning. Levensgevaar. Peligro de Muerte. Electricidad. Danger. Give me my spear. Old father, old artificer, stand me now and ever in good stead. You like this garden? Why is it yours? We evict those who destroy! And then went down to the ship, set keel to breakers, forth on the godly sea. There is no "official" theory of time, defined in creeds or universally agreed upon among Christians. Christianity is not concerned with the purely scientific aspects of the subject nor, within wide limits, with its philosophical analysis, except insofar as it is committed to a fundamentally realist view and could not admit, as some Eastern philosophies have done, that temporal existence is mere illusion. A shudder in the loins engenders there the broken wall, the burning roof and tower and Agamemnon dead. Stately, plump Buck Mulligan came from the stairhead, bearing a bowl of lather on which a mirror and a razor lay crossed. In what distant deeps or skies burnt the fire of thine eyes? On what wings dare he aspire?

What the hand dare seize the fire? These fragments I have shored against my ruins. Hieronymo's mad again. Then felt I like some watcher of the skies when a new planet swims into his ken. It has also lately been postulated that the physical concept of information is identical with a phenomenon of reversal of entropy. The psychologist must add a few remarks here: It does not seem convincing to me that information is eo ipso identical with a pouvoir d'organisation which undoes entropy. Datta. Dayadhvam. Damyata. Shantih shantih shantih.

Nevertheless, once the ship is past Scylla and slowing toward the Abbondanza planets, the periods of fugue become frequent once again, so that he lives entrapped, shuttling between the flashing shadows of yesterday and tomorrow.

* * * *

After the Coustakis overload he tried to go on in the old way, as best he could. He gave Coustakis a refund without even being asked, for he had been of no service, nor could he ever be. Instantaneous transportation of matter would have to wait. But Skein took other clients. He could still make the communion, after a fashion, and when the nature of the task was sufficiently low-level he could even deliver a decent synergetic response.

Often his work was unsatisfactory, however. Contacts would break at awkward moments, or, conversely, his filter mechanism would weaken and he would allow the entire contents of his client's mind to flow into that of his consultant. The results of such disasters were chaotic, involving him in heavy medical expenses and sometimes in damage suits. He was forced to place his fees on a contingency basis: no synergy, no pay. About half the time he earned nothing for his output of energy. Meanwhile his overhead remained the same as always: the domed office, the network of consultants, the research staff, and the rest. His effort to remain in business was eating rapidly into the bank accounts he had set aside against just such a time of storm.

They could find no organic injury to his brain. Of course, so little was known about a Communicator's gift that it was impossible to determine much by medical analysis. If they could not locate the centre center from which a Communicator powered his communions, how could they detect the place where he had been hurt? The medical archives were of no value; there had been eleven previous cases of overload, but each instance was physiologically unique. They told him he would eventually heal, and sent him away. Sometimes the doctors gave him silly therapies: counting exercises, rhythmic blinkings, hopping on his left leg and then his right, as if he had a stroke. But he had not had a stroke.

For a time he was able to maintain his business on the momentum of his reputation. Then, as word got around that he had been hurt and was no longer any good, clients stopped coming. Even the contingency basis for fees failed to attract them. Within six months he found that he was lucky to find a client a week. He reduced his rates, and that seemed only to make things worse, so he raised them to something not far below what they had been at the time of the overload. For a while the pace of business increased, as if people were getting the impression that Skein had recovered. He gave such spotty service, though. Blurred and wavering communions, unanticipated positive feedbacks, filtering problems, information deficiencies, redundancy surpluses—"You take your mind in your hands when you go to Skein," they were saying now.

The fugues added to his professional difficulties.

He never knew when he would snap into hallucination. It might happen during a communion, and often did. Once he dropped back to the moment of the Coustakis-Nissenson hookup and treated a terrified client to a replay of his overload. Once, although he did not understand at the time what was happening, he underwent a flashforward and carried the client with him to a scarlet jungle on a formaldehyde world, and when Skein slipped back to reality the client remained in the scarlet jungle. There was a damage suit over that one, too.

Temporal dislocation plagued him into making poor guesses. He took on clients whom he could not possibly serve and wasted his time on them. He turned away people whom he might have been able to help to his own profit. Since he was no longer anchored firmly to his timeline, but drifted in random oscillations of twenty years or more in either direction, he forfeited the keen sense of perspective on which he had previously founded his professional judgments. He grew haggard and lean, also. He passed through a tempest of spiritual doubts that amounted to total submission and then total rejection of faith within the course of four months. He changed lawyers almost weekly. He liquidated assets with invariably catastrophic timing to pay his cascading bills.

A year and a half after the overload, he formally renounced his registration and closed his office. It took six months more to settle the remaining damage suits. Then, with what was left of his money, he bought a spaceliner ticket and set out to search for a world with purple sand and blue-leaved trees, where, unless his fugues had played him false, he might be able to arrange for the repair of his broken mind.

* * * *

Now the ship has returned to the conventional fourspace and dawdles planetward at something rather less than half the speed of light. Across the screens there spreads a necklace of stars; space is crowded here. The captain will point out Abbondanza to anyone who asks: a lemon-colored sun, bigger than that of Earth, surrounded by a dozen bright planetary pips. The passengers are excited. They buzz, twitter, speculate, anticipate. No one is silent except Skein. He is aware of many love affairs; he has had to reject several offers just in the past three days. He has given up reading and is trying to purge his mind of all he has stuffed into it. The fugues have grown worse. He has to write notes to himself, saying things like You are a passenger aboard a ship heading for Abbondanza VI, and will be landing in a few days, so that he does not forget which of his three entangled timelines is the true one.

* * * *

Suddenly he is with Nilla on the island in the Gulf of Mexico, getting aboard the little excursion boat. Time stands still here; it could almost be the twentieth century. The frayed, sagging cords of the rigging. The lumpy engine inefficiently converted from internal combustion to turbines. The mustachioed Mexican bandits who will be their guides today. Nilla, nervously coiling her long blonde hair, saying, "Will I get seasick, John? The boat rides right in the water, doesn't it? It won't even hover a little bit?"

"Terribly archaic," Skein says. "That's why we're here."

The captain gestures them aboard. Juan, Francisco, Sebastián. Brothers. Los hermanos. Yards of white teeth glistening below the drooping moustaches. With a terrible roar the boat moves away from the dock. Soon the little town of crumbling pastel buildings is out of sight and they are heading jaggedly eastward along the coast, green shoreward water on their left, the blue depths on the right. The morning sun coming up hard. "Could I sunbathe?" Nilla asks. Unsure of herself; he has never seen her this way, so hesitant, so abashed. Mexico has robbed her of her New York assurance. "Go ahead," Skein says. "Why not?" She drops her robe. Underneath she wears only a waist-strap; her heavy breasts look white and vulnerable in the tropic glare, and the small nipples are a faded pink. Skein sprays her with protective sealant and she sprawls out on the deck. Los hermanos stare hungrily and talk to each other in low rumbling tones. Not Spanish. Mayan, perhaps? The natives have never learned to adopt the tourists' casual nudity here. Nilla, obviously still uneasy, rolls over and lies face down. Her broad smooth back glistens.

Juan and Francisco yell. Skein follows their pointing fingers. Porpoises! A dozen of them, frisking around the bow, keeping just ahead of the boat, leaping high and slicing down into the blue water. Nilla gives a little cry of joy and rushes to the side to get a closer look. Throwing her arm self-consciously across her bare breasts. "You don't need to do that," Skein murmurs. She keeps herself covered. "How lovely they are," she says softly. Sebastián comes up beside them. "Amigos," he says. "They are. My friends." The cavorting porpoises eventually disappear. The boat bucks bouncily onward, keeping close to the island's beautiful empty palmy shore. Later they anchor, and he and Nilla swim masked, spying on the coral gardens. When they haul themselves on deck again it is almost noon. The sun is terrible. "Lunch?" Francisco asks. "We make you good lunch now?" Nilla laughs. She is no longer hiding her body. "I'm starved!" she cries.

"We make you good lunch," Francisco says, grinning, and he and Juan go over the side. In the shallow water they are clearly visible near the white sand of the bottom. They have spear guns; they hold their breaths and prowl. Too late Skein realizes what they are doing. Francisco hauls a fluttering spiny lobster out from behind a rock. Juan impales a huge pale crab. He grabs three conchs also, surfaces, dumps his prey on the deck. Francisco arrives with the lobster. Juan, below again, spears a second lobster. The animals are not dead; they crawl sadly in circles on the deck as they dry. Appalled, Skein turns to Sebastián and says, "Tell them to stop. We're not that hungry." Sebastián, preparing some kind of salad, smiles and shrugs. Francisco has brought up another crab, bigger than the first. "Enough," Skein says. "Basta! Basta!" Juan, dripping, tosses down three more conchs. "You pay us good," he says. "We give you good lunch." Skein shakes his head. The deck is becoming a slaughterhouse for ocean life. Sebastián now energetically slits conch shells, extracts the meat, drops it into a vast bowl to marinate in a yellow-green fluid. "Basta!" Skein yells: Is that the right word in Spanish? He knows it's right in Italian. Los hermanos look amused. The sea is full of life, they seem to be telling him. We give you good lunch. Suddenly Francisco erupts from the water, bearing something immense. A turtle! Forty, fifty pounds! The joke has gone too far. "No," Skein says. "Listen, I have to forbid this. Those turtles are almost extinct. Do you understand that? Muerto. Perdido. Desaparecido. I won't eat a turtle. Throw it back. Throw it back." Francisco smiles. He shakes his head. Deftly he binds the turtle's flippers with rope. Juan says, "Not for lunch, señor. For us. For to sell. Mucho dinero." Skein can do nothing. Francisco and Sebastián have begun to hack up the crabs and lobsters. Juan slices peppers into the bowl where the conchs are marinating. Pieces of dead animals litter the deck. "Oh, I'm starving," Nilla says. Her waist-strap is off too, now. The turtle watches the whole scene, beady-eyed. Skein shudders. Auschwitz, he thinks. Buchenwald. For the animals it's Buchenwald every day.

* * * *

Purple sand, blue-leaved trees. An orange sea gleaming not far to the west under a lemon sun. "It isn't much farther," the skull-faced man says. "You can make it. Step by step by step is how."

"I'm winded," Skein says. "Those hills—"

"I'm twice your age, and I'm doing fine."

"You're in better shape. I've been cooped up on spaceships for months and months."

"Just a short way on," says the skull-faced man. "About a hundred meters from the shore."

Skein struggles on. The heat is frightful. He has trouble getting a footing in the shifting sand. Twice he trips over black vines whose fleshy runners form a mat a few centimeters under the surface; loops of the vines stick up here and there. He even suffers a brief fugue, a seven-second flashback to a day in Jerusalem. Somewhere at the core of his mind he is amused by that: a flashback within a flashforward. Encapsulated concentric hallucinations. When he comes out of it, he finds himself getting to his feet and brushing sand from his clothing. Ten steps onward the skull-faced man halts him and says, "There it is. Look there, in the pit."

Skein sees a funnel-shaped crater right in front of him, perhaps five meters in diameter at ground level and dwindling to about half that width at its bottom, some six or seven meters down. The pit strikes him as a series of perfect circles making up a truncated cone. Its sides are smooth and firm, almost glazed, and the sand has a brown tinge. In the pit, resting peacefully on the flat floor, is something that looks like a golden amoeba the size of a large cat. A row of round blue-black eyes crosses the hump of its back. From the perimeter of its body comes a soft green radiance.

"Go down to it," the skull-faced man says. "The force of its power falls off with the cube of the distance; from up here you can't feel it. Go down. Let it take you over. Fuse with it. Make communion, Skein, make communion!"

"And will it heal me? So that I'll function as I did before the trouble started?"

"If you let it heal you, it will. That's what it wants to do. It's a completely benign organism. It thrives on repairing broken souls. Let it into your head, let it find the damaged place. You can trust it. Go down."

Skein trembles on the edge of the pit. The creature below flows and eddies, becoming first long and narrow, then high and squat, then resuming its basically circular form. Its color deepens almost to scarlet, and its radiance shifts toward yellow. As if preening and stretching itself. It seems to be waiting for him. It seems eager. This is what he has sought so long, going from planet to wearying planet. The skull-faced man, the purple sand, the pit, the creature. Skein slips his sandals off. What have I to lose? He sits for a moment on the pit's rim; then he shimmies down, sliding part of the way, and lands softly, close beside the being that awaits him. And immediately feels its power.

* * * *

He enters the huge desolate cavern that is the cathedral of Haghia Sophia. A few Turkish guides lounge hopefully against the vast marble pillars. Tourists shuffle about, reading to each other from cheap plastic guidebooks. A shaft of light enters from some improbable aperture and splinters against the Moslem pulpit. It seems to Skein that he hears the tolling of bells and feels incense prickling at his nostrils. But how can that be? No Christian rites have been performed here in a thousand years. A Turk looms before him. "Show you the mosyics?" he says. Mosyics. "Help you understand this marvelous building? A dollar. No? Maybe change money? A good rate. Dollars, marks, Eurocredits, what? You speak English? Show you the mosyics?" The Turk fades. The bells grow louder. A row of bowed priests in white silk robes files past the altar, chanting in—what? Greek? The ceiling is encrusted with gems. Gold plate gleams everywhere. Skein senses the terrible complexity of the cathedral, teeming now with life, a whole universe engulfed in this gloom, a thousand chapels packed with worshippers, long lines waiting to urinate in the crypts, a marketplace in the balcony, jeweled necklaces changing hands with low murmurs of negotiation, babies being born behind the alabaster sarcophagi, the bells tolling, dukes nodding to one another, clouds of incense swirling toward the dome, the figures in the mosaics alive, making the sign of the Cross, smiling, blowing kisses, the pillars moving now, becoming fat-middled as they bend from side to side, the entire colossal structure shifting and flowing and melting. And a ballet of Turks. "Show you the mosyics?" "Change money?" "Postcards? Souvenir of Istanbul?" A plump, pink American face: "You're John Skein, aren't you? The Communicator? We worked together on the big fusion-chamber merger in '53." Skein shakes his head. "It must be that you are mistaken," he says, speaking in Italian. "I am not he. Pardon. Pardon." And joins the line of chanting priests.

* * * *

Purple sand, blue-leaved trees. An orange sea under a lemon sun. Looking out from the top deck of the terminal, an hour after landing, Skein sees a row of towering hotels rising along the nearby beach. At once he feels the wrongness: there should be no hotels. The right planet has no such towers; therefore this is another of the wrong ones.

He suffers from complete disorientation as he attempts to place himself in sequence. Where am I? Aboard a liner heading toward Abbondanza VI. What do I see? A world I have previously visited. Which one? The one with the hotels. The third out of seven, isn't it?

He has seen this planet before, in flashforwards. Long before he left Earth to begin his quest he glimpsed those hotels, that beach. Now he views it in flashback. That perplexes him. He must try to see himself as a moving point travelling through time, viewing the scenery now from this perspective, now from that.

He watches his earlier self at the terminal. Once it was his future self. How confusing, how needlessly muddling! "I'm looking for an old Earthman," he says. "He must be a hundred, hundred-twenty years old. A face like a skull—no flesh at all, really. A brittle man. No? Well, can you tell me, does this planet have a life-form about this big, a kind of blob of golden jelly, that lives in pits down by the seashore, and—no? No? Ask someone else, you say? Of course. And perhaps a hotel room? As long as I've come all this way."

He is getting tired of finding the wrong planets. What folly this is, squandering his last savings on a quest for a world seen in a dream! He would have expected planets with purple sand and blue-leaved trees to be uncommon, but no, in an infinite universe one can find a dozen of everything, and now he has wasted almost half his money and close to a year, visiting two planets and this one and not finding what he seeks.

He goes to the hotel they arrange for him.

The beach is packed with sunbathers, most of them from Earth. Skein walks among them. "Look," he wants to say, "I have this trouble with my brain, an old injury, and it gives me these visions of myself in the past and future, and one of the visions I see is a place where there's a skull-faced man who takes me to a kind of amoeba in a pit that can heal me, do you follow? And it's a planet with purple sand and blue-leaved trees, just like this one, and I figure if I keep going long enough I'm bound to find it and the skull-face and the amoeba, do you follow me? And maybe this is the planet after all, only I'm in the wrong part of it. What should I do? What hope do you think I really have?" This is the third world. He knows that he must visit a number of wrong ones before he finds the right one. But how many? How many? And when will he know that he has the right one?

Standing silent on the beach, he feels confusion come over him, and drops into fugue, and is hurled to another world. Purple sand, blue-leaved trees. A fat, friendly Pingalorian consul. "A skull-faced man? No, I can't say I know of any." Which world is this, Skein wonders? One that I have already visited, or one that I have not yet come to? The manifold layers of illusion dazzle him. Past and future and present lie like a knot around his throat. Shifting planes of reality; intersecting films of event. Purple sand, blue-leaved trees. Which planet is this? Which one? Which one? He is back on the crowded beach. A lemon sun. An orange sea. He is back in his cabin on the spaceliner. He sees a note in his own handwriting: You are a passenger aboard a ship heading for Abbondanza VI, and will be landing in a few days. So everything was a vision. Flashback? Flashforward? He is no longer able to tell. He is baffled by these identical worlds. Purple sand. Blue-leaved trees. He wishes he knew how to cry.

* * * *

Instead of a client and a consultant for today's communion, Skein has a client and a client. A man and a woman, Michaels and Miss Schumpeter. The communion is of an unusually intimate kind. Michaels has been married six times, and several of the marriages apparently have been dissolved under bitter circumstances. Miss Schumpeter, a woman of some wealth, loves Michaels but doesn't entirely trust him; she wants a peep into his mind before she'll put her thumb to the marital cube. Skein will oblige. The fee has already been credited to his account. Let me not to the marriage of true minds admit impediments. If she does not like what she finds in her beloved's soul, there may not be any marriage, but Skein will have been paid.

A tendril of his mind goes to Michaels, now. A tendril to Miss Schumpeter. Skein opens his filters. "Now you'll meet for the first time," he tells them. Michaels flows to her. Miss Schumpeter flows to him. Skein is merely the conduit.

Through him pass the ambitions, betrayals, failures, vanities, deteriorations, disputes, treacheries, lusts, generosities, shames, and follies of these two human beings. If he wishes, he can examine the most private sins of Miss Schumpeter and the darkest yearnings of her future husband. But he does not care. He sees such things every day. He takes no pleasure in spying on the psyches of these two. Would a surgeon grow excited over the sight of Miss Schumpeter's Fallopian tubes or Michaels's pancreas? Skein is merely doing his job. He is no voyeur, simply a Communicator. He looks upon himself as a public utility.

When he severs the contact, Miss Schumpeter and Michaels both are weeping.

"I love you!" she wails.

"Get away from me!" he mutters.

* * * *

Purple sand. Blue-leaved trees. Oily orange sea.

The skull-faced man says, "Won't you ever come to see that causality is merely an illusion, Skein? The notion that there's a consecutive series of events is nothing but a fraud. We impose form on our lives, we talk of time's arrow, we say that there's a flow from A through G and Q to Z, we make believe everything is nicely linear. But it isn't, Skein. It isn't."

"So you keep telling me."

"I feel an obligation to awaken your mind to the truth. G can come before A, and Z before both of them. Most of us don't like to perceive it that way, so we arrange things in what seems like a more logical pattern, just as a novelist will put the motive before the murder and the murder before the arrest. But the universe isn't a novel. We can't make nature imitate art. It's all random, Skein, random, random!"

* * * *

"Half a million?"

"Half a million."

"You know I don't have that kind of money."

"Let's not waste time, Mr. Coustakis. You have assets. Pledge them as collateral. Credit is easily obtained." Skein waits for the inventor to clear his loan. "Now we can proceed," he says, and tells his desk, "Get Nissenson into a receptive state."

Coustakis says, "First let me get it clear. This man will see everything that's in my mind? He'll get access to my secrets?"

"No. No. I filter the communion with great care. Nothing will pass from your mind to his except the nature of the problem you want him to tackle. Nothing will came come back from his mind to yours except the answer."

"And if he doesn't have the answer?"

"He will."

"And if he goes into the transmission business for himself afterward?"

"He's bonded," Skein says curtly. "No chance of it. Let's go, now. Up and together."

"Skein? Skein? Skein? Skein?"

* * * *

The wind is rising. The sand, blown aloft, stains the sky grey. Skein clambers from the pit and lies by its rim, breathing hard. The skull-faced man helps him get up.

Skein has seen this series of images hundreds of times. "How do you feel?" the skull-faced man asks.

"Strange. Good. My head seems so clear!"

"You had communion down there?"

"Oh, yes. Yes."

"And?"

"I think I'm healed," Skein says in wonder. "My strength is back. Before, you know, I felt cut down to the bone, a minimum version of myself. And now. And now." He lets a tendril of consciousness slip forth. It meets the mind of the skull-faced man. Skein is aware of a glassy interface; he can touch the other mind, but he cannot enter it. "Are you a Communicator too?" Skein asks, awed.

"In a sense. I feel you touching me. You're better, aren't you?"

"Much. Much. Much."

"As I told you. Now you have your second chance, Skein. Your gift has been restored. Courtesy of our friend in the pit. They love being helpful."

"Skein? Skein? Skein? Skein?"

* * * *

We conceive of time either as flowing or as enduring. The problem is how to reconcile these concepts. From a purely formalistic point of view there exists no difficulty, as these properties can be reconciled by means of the concept of a duratio successiva. Every unit of time measure has this characteristic of a flowing permanence: an hour streams by while it lasts and so long as it lasts. Its flowing is thus identical with its duration. Time, from this point of view, is transitory; but its passing away lasts.

* * * *

In the early months of his affliction he experienced a great many scenes of flashforward while in fugue. He saw himself outside the nineteenth-century mansion, he saw himself in a dozen lawyers' offices, he saw himself in hotels, terminals, spaceliners, he saw himself discussing the nature of time with the skull-faced man, he saw himself trembling on the edge of the pit, he saw himself emerging healed, he saw himself wandering from world to world, looking for the right one with purple sand and blue-leaved trees. As time unfolded most of these flash-forwards duly entered the flow of the present; he did come to the mansion, he did go to those hotels and terminals, he did wander those useless worlds. Now, as he approaches Abbondanza VI, he goes through a great many flashbacks and a relatively few flashforwards, and the flashforwards seem to be limited to a fairly narrow span of time, covering his landing on Abbondanza VI, his first meeting with the skull-faced man, his journey to the pit, and his emergence, healed, from the amoeba's lair. Never anything beyond that final scene. He wonders if time is going to run out for him on Abbondanza VI.

The ship lands on Abbondanza VI half a day ahead of schedule. There are the usual decontamination procedures to endure, and while they are going on Skein rests in his cabin, counting minutes to liberty. He is curiously confident that this will be the world on which he finds the skull-faced man and the benign amoeba. Of course, he has felt that way before, looking out from other spaceliners at other planets of the proper coloration, and he has been wrong. But the intensity of his confidence is something new. He is sure that the end of his quest lies here.

"Debarkation beginning now," the loudspeakers say.

He joins the line of outgoing passengers. The others smile, embrace, whisper; they have found friends or even mates on this voyage. He remains apart. No one says goodbye to him. He emerges into a brightly lit terminal, a great cube of glass that looks like all the other terminals scattered across the thousands of worlds that man has reached. He could be in Chicago or Johannesburg or Beirut: the scene is one of porters, reservations clerks, customs officials, hotel agents, taxi drivers, guides. A blight of sameness spreading across the universe. Stumbling through the customs gate, Skein finds himself set upon. Does he want a taxi, a hotel room, a woman, a man, a guide, a homestead plot, a servant, a ticket to Abbondanza VII, a private car, an interpreter, a bank, a telephone? The hubbub jolts Skein into three consecutive ten-second fugues, all flashbacks; he sees a rainy day in Tierra del Fuego, he conducts a communion to help a maker of sky-spectacles perfect the plot of his latest extravaganza, and he puts his palm to a cube in order to dictate contract terms to Nicholas Coustakis. Then Coustakis fades, the terminal reappears, and Skein realizes that someone has seized him by the left arm just above the elbow. Bony fingers dig painfully into his flesh. It is the skull-faced man. "Come with me," he says. "I'll take you where you want to go."

"This isn't just another flashforward, is it?" Skein asks, as he has watched himself ask so many times in the past. "I mean you're really here to get me."

The skull-faced man says, as Skein has heard him say so many times in the past, "No, this time it's no flashforward. I'm really here to get you."

"Thank God. Thank God. Thank God."

"Follow along this way. You have your passport handy?"

The familiar words. Skein is prepared to discover he is merely in fugue, and expects to drop back into frustrating reality at any moment. But no. The scene does not waver. It holds firm. It holds. At last he has caught up with this particular scene, overtaking it and enclosing it, pearl-like, in the folds of the present. He is on the way out of the terminal. The skull-faced man helps him through the formalities. How withered he is! How fiery the eyes, how gaunt the face! Those frightening orbits of bone jutting through the skin of the forehead. That parched cheek. Skein listens for a dry rattle of ribs. One sturdy punch and there would be nothing left but a cloud of white dust, slowly settling.

"I know your difficulty," the skull-faced man says. "You've been caught in entropy's jaws. You're being devoured. The injury to your mind—it's tipped you into a situation you aren't able to handle. You could handle it, if you'd only learn to adapt to the nature of the perceptions you're getting now. But you won't do that, will you? And you want to be healed. Well, you can be healed here, all right. More or less healed. I'll take you to the place."

"What do you mean, I could handle it, if I'd only learn to adapt?"

"Your injury has liberated you. It's shown you the truth about time. But you refuse to see it."

"What truth?" Skein asks flatly.

"You still try to think that time flows neatly from alpha to omega, from yesterday through today to tomorrow," the skull-faced man says, as they walk slowly through the terminal. "But it doesn't. The idea of the forward flow of time is a deception we impose on ourselves in childhood. An abstraction, agreed upon by common convention, to make it easier for us to cope with phenomena. The truth is that events are random, that chronological flow is only our joint hallucination, that if time can be said to flow at all, it flows in all 'directions' at once. Therefore—"

"Wait," Skein says. "How do you explain the laws of thermodynamics? Entropy increases, available energy constantly diminishes, the universe heads toward ultimate stasis."

"Does it?"

"The second law of thermodynamics—"

"Is an abstraction," the skull-faced man says, "which unfortunately fails to correspond with the situation in the true universe. It isn't a divine law. It's a mathematical hypothesis developed by men who weren't able to perceive the real situation. They did their best to account for the data within a framework they could understand. Their laws are formulations of probability, based on conditions that hold within closed systems, and given the right closed system the second law is useful and illuminating. But in the universe as a whole it simply isn't true. There is no arrow of time. Entropy does not necessarily increase. Natural processes can be reversible. Causes do not invariably precede effects. In fact, the concepts of cause and effect are empty. There are neither causes nor effects, but only events, spontaneously generated, which we arrange in our minds in comprehensible patterns of sequence."

"No," Skein mutters. "This is insanity!"

"There are no patterns. Everything is random."

"No."

"Why not admit it? Your brain has been injured. What was destroyed was the centre center of temporal perception, the node that humans use to impose this unreal order on events. Your time filter has burned out. The past and the future are as accessible to you as the present, Skein: you can go where you like, you can watch events drifting past as they really do. Only you haven't been able to break up your old habits of thought. You still try to impose the conventional entropic order on things, even though you lack the mechanism to do it, now, and the conflict between what you perceive and what you think you perceive is driving you crazy. Eh?"

"How do you know so much about me?"

The skull-faced man chuckles. "I was injured in the same way as you. I was cut free from the timeline long ago, through the kind of overload you suffered. And I've had years to come to terms with the new reality. I was as terrified as you were, at first. But now I understand. I move about freely. I know things, Skein." A rasping laugh. "You need rest, though. A room, a bed. Time to think things over. Come. There's no rush now. You're on the right planet; you'll be all right soon."

* * * *

Further, the association of entropy increase with time's arrow is in no sense circular; rather, it both tells us something about what will happen to natural systems in time, and about what the time order must be for a series of states of a system. Thus, we may often establish a time order among a set of events by use of the time-entropy association, free from any reference to clocks and magnitudes of time intervals from the present. In actual judgments of before-after we frequently do this on the basis of our experience (even though without any explicit knowledge of the law of entropy increase): we know, for example, that for iron in air the state of pure metal must have been before that of a rusted surface, or that the clothes will be dry after, not before, they have hung in the hot sun.

* * * *

A tense, humid night of thunder and temporal storms. Lying alone in his oversize hotel room, five kilometers from the purple shore, Skein suffers fiercely from fugue.

* * * *

"Listen, I have to forbid this. Those turtles are almost extinct. Do you understand that? Muerto. Perdido. Desaparecido. I won't eat a turtle. Throw it back. Throw it back."

* * * *

"I'm happy to say your second go-round has been approved, Mr. Skein. Not that there was ever any doubt. A long and happy new life to you, sir."

* * * *

"Go down to it. The force of its power falls off with the cube of the distance; from up here you can't feel it. Go down. Let it take you over. Fuse with it. Make communion, Skein, make communion!"

* * * *

"Show you the mosyics? Help you understand this marvelous building? A dollar. No? Maybe change money? A good rate."

* * * *

"First let me get it clear. This man will see everything that's in my mind? He'll get access to my secrets?"

* * * *

"I love you."

"Get away from me!"

* * * *

"Won't you ever come to see that causality is merely an illusion, Skein? The notion that there's a consecutive series of events is nothing but a fraud. We impose form on our lives, we talk of time's arrow, we say that there's a flow from A through G and Q to Z, we make believe everything is nicely linear. But it isn't, Skein. It isn't."

* * * *

Breakfast on a leafy veranda. Morning light out of the west, making the trees glow with an ultramarine glitter. The skull-faced man joins him. Skein secretly searches the parched face. Is everything an illusion? Perhaps he is an illusion.

They walk toward the sea. Well before noon they reach the shore. The skull-faced man points to the south, and they follow the coast; it is often a difficult hike, for in places the sand is washed out and they must detour inland, scrambling over quartzy cliffs. The monstrous old man is indefatigable.

When they pause to rest, squatting on a timeless purple strand made smooth by the recent tide, the debate about time resumes, and Skein hears words that have been echoing in his skull for four years and more. It is as though everything up till now has been a rehearsal for a play, and now at last he has taken the stage.

"Won't you ever come to see that causality is merely an illusion, Skein?"

"I feel an obligation to awaken your mind to the truth."

"Time is an ocean, and events come drifting to us as randomly as dead animals on the waves."

Skein offers all the proper cues.

"I won't accept that! It's demonic, chaotic, nihilistic theory."

"You can say that after all you've experienced?"

"I'll go on saying it. What I've been going through is a mental illness. Maybe I'm deranged, but the universe isn't."

"Contrary. You've only recently become sane and started to see things as they really are. The trouble is that you don't want to admit the evidence you've begun to perceive. Your filters are down, Skein! You've shaken free of the illusion of linearity! Now's your chance to show your resilience. Learn to live with the real reality. Stop this silly business of imposing an artificial order on the flow of time. Why should effect follow cause? Why shouldn't the seed follow the tree? Why must you persist in holding tight to a useless, outworn, contemptible system of false evaluations of experience when you've managed to break free of the—"

"Stop it! Stop it! Stop it! Stop it!"

* * * *

By early afternoon they are many kilometers from the hotel, still keeping as close to the shore as they can. The terrain is uneven and divided, with rugged fingers of rock running almost to the water's edge, and Skein finds the journey even more exhausting than it had seemed in his visions of it. Several times he stops, panting, and has to be urged to go on.

"It isn't much farther," the skull-faced man says. "You can make it. Step by step is how."

"I'm winded. Those hills—"

"I'm twice your age, and I'm doing fine."

"You're in better shape. I've been cooped up on spaceships for months and months."

"Just a short way on," says the skull-faced man. "About a hundred meters from the shore."

Skein struggles on. The heat is frightful. He trips in the sand; he is blinded by sweat; he has a momentary flashback fugue. "There it is," the skull-faced man says finally. "Look there, in the pit."

Skein beholds the conical crater. He sees the golden amoeba

"Go down to it," the skull-faced man says. "The force of its power falls off with the cube of the distance; from up here you can't feel it. Go down. Let it take you over. Fuse with it. Make communion, Skein, make communion!"

"And will it heal me? So that I'll function as I did before the trouble started?"

"If you let it heal you, it will. That's what it wants to do. It's a completely benign organism. It thrives on repairing broken souls. Let it into your head; let it find the damaged place. You can trust it. Go down."

Skein trembles on the edge of the pit. The creature below flows and eddies, becoming first long and narrow, then high and squat, then resuming its basically circular form. Its color deepens almost to scarlet, and its radiance shifts toward yellow. As if preening and stretching itself. It seems to be waiting for him. It seems eager. This is what he has sought so long, going from planet to wearying planet. The skull-faced man, the purple sand, the pit, the creature. Skein slips his sandals off. What have I to lose? He sits for a moment on the pit's rim; then he shimmies down, sliding part of the way, and lands softly, close beside the being that awaits him. And immediately feels its power. Something brushes against his brain. The sensation reminds him of the training sessions of his first go-round, when the instructors were showing him how to develop his gift. The fingers probing his consciousness. Go on, enter, he tells them. I'm open. And he finds himself in contact with the being of the pit. Wordless. A two-way flow of unintelligible images is the only communion; shapes drift from and into his mind. The universe blurs. He is no longer sure where the center of his ego lies. He has thought of his brain as a sphere with himself at its center, but now it seems extended, elliptical, and an ellipse has no center, only a pair of focuses, here and here, one focus in his own skull and one—where?—within that fleshy amoeba. And suddenly he is looking at himself through the amoeba's eyes. The large biped with the bony body. How strange, how grotesque! Yet it suffers. Yet it must be helped. It is injured. It is broken. We go to it with all our love. We will heal. And Skein feels something flowing over the bare folds and fissures of his brain. But he can no longer remember whether he is the human or the alien, the bony one or the boneless. Their identities have mingled. He goes through fugues by the scores, seeing yesterdays and tomorrows, and everything is formless and without content; he is unable to recognize himself or to understand the words being spoken. It does not matter. All is random. All is illusion. Release the knot of pain you clutch within you. Accept. Accept. Accept. Accept.

He accepts.

He releases.

He merges.

He casts away the shreds of ego, the constricting exoskeleton of self, and placidly permits the necessary adjustments to be made.

* * * *

The possibility, however, of genuine thermodynamic entropy decrease for an isolated system—no matter how rare—does raise an objection to the definition of time's direction in terms of entropy. If a large, isolated system did by chance go through an entropy decrease as one state evolved from another, we would have to say that time "went backward" if our definition of time's arrow were basically in terms of entropy increase. But with an ultimate definition of the forward direction of time in terms of the actual occurrence of states, and measured time intervals from the present, we can readily accommodate the entropy decrease; it would become merely a rare anomaly in the physical processes of the natural world.

* * * *

The wind is rising. The sand, blown aloft, stains the sky grey. Skein clambers from the pit and lies by its rim, breathing hard. The skull-faced man helps him get up.

Skein has seen this series of images hundreds of times. "How do you feel?" the skull-faced man asks.

"Strange. Good. My head seems clear!"

"You had communion down there?"

"Oh, yes. Yes."

"And?"

"I think I'm healed," Skein says in wonder. "My strength is back. Before, you know, I felt cut down to the bone, a minimum version of myself. And now. And now." He lets a tendril of consciousness slip forth. It meets the mind of the skull-faced man. Skein is aware of a glassy interface; he can touch the other mind, but he cannot enter it. "Are you a Communicator too?" Skein asks, awed.

"In a sense. I feel you touching me. You're better, aren't you?"

"Much. Much. Much."

"As I told you. Now you have your second chance, Skein. Your gift has been restored. Courtesy of our friend in the pit. They love being helpful."

"What shall I do now? Where shall I go?"

"Anything. Anywhere. Anywhen. You're free to move along the timeline as you please. In a state of controlled, directed fugue, so to speak. After all, if time is random, if there is no rigid sequence of events—"

"Yes."

"Then why not choose the sequence that appeals to you? Why stick to the set of abstractions your former self has handed you? You're a free man, Skein. Go. Enjoy. Undo your past. Edit it. Improve on it. It isn't your past, any more than this is your present. It's all one, Skein, all one. Pick the segment you prefer."

He tests the truth of the skull-faced man's words. Cautiously Skein steps three minutes into the past and sees himself struggling up out of the pit. He slides four minutes into the future and sees the skull-faced man, alone, trudging northward along the shore. Everything flows. All is fluidity. He is free. He is free.

"You see, Skein?"

"Now I do," Skein says. He is out of entropy's jaws. He is time's master, which is to say he is his own master. He can move at will. He can defy the imaginary forces of determinism. Suddenly he realizes what he must do now. He will assert his free will; he will challenge entropy on its home ground. Skein smiles. He cuts free of the timeline and floats easily into what others would call the past.

"Get Nissenson into a receptive state," he orders his desk.

Coustakis, blinking rapidly, obviously uneasy, says, "First let me get it clear. This man will see everything that's in my mind? He'll get access to my secrets?"

"No. No. I filter the communion with great care. Nothing will pass from your mind to his except the nature of the problem you want him to tackle. Nothing will come back from his mind to yours except the answer."

"And if he doesn't have the answer?"

"He will."

"And if he goes into the transmission business for himself afterward?" Coustakis asks.

"He's bonded," Skein says curtly. "No chance of it. Let's go, now. Up and together."

The desk reports that Nissenson, half the world away in São Paulo, is ready. Quickly Skein throws Coustakis into the receptive condition, and swings around to face the brilliant lights of his data-access units. Here is the moment when he can halt the transaction. Turn again, Skein. Face Coustakis, smile sadly, inform him that the communion will be impossible. Give him back his money, send him off to break some other Communicator's mind. And live on, whole and happy, ever after. It was at this point, visiting this scene endlessly in his fugues, that Skein silently and hopelessly cried out to himself to stop. Now it is within his power, for this is no fugue, no illusion of time-shift. He has shifted. He is here, carrying with him the knowledge of all that is to come, and he is the only Skein on the scene, the operative Skein. Get up, now. Refuse the contract.

He does not. Thus he defies entropy. Thus he breaks the chain.

He peers into the sparkling, shifting little blazes until they kindle his gift, jabbing at the electrical rhythms of his brain until he is lifted into the energy level that permits the opening of a communion. He starts to go up. He reaches forth one tendril of his mind and engages Nissenson. With another tendril he snares Coustakis. Steadily, now, he draws the two tendrils together. He is aware of the risks, but believes he can surmount them.

The tendrils meet.

Out of Coustakis's mind flows a description of the matter transmitter and a clear statement of the beam-spread problem; Skein shoves it along to Nissenson, who begins to work on a solution. The combined strength of the two minds is great, but Skein deftly lets the excess charge bleed away and maintains the communion with no particular effort, holding Coustakis and Nissenson together while they deal with their technical matters. Skein pays little attention as their excited minds rush toward answers. If you. Yes, and then. But if. I see, yes. I could. And. However, maybe I should. I like that. It leads to. Of course. The inevitable result. Is it feasible, though? I think so. You might have to. I could. Yes. I could. I could.

"I thank you a million times," Coustakis says to Skein. "It was all so simple, once we saw how we ought to look at it. I don't begrudge your fee at all. Not at all."

Coustakis leaves, glowing with delight. Skein, relieved, tells his desk, "I'm going to allow myself a three-day holiday. Fix the schedule to move everybody up accordingly."

He smiles. He strides across his office, turning up the amplifiers, treating himself to the magnificent view. The nightmare undone. The past revised. The burnout avoided. All it took was confidence. Enlightenment. A proper understanding of the processes involved.

He feels the sudden swooping sensations of incipient temporal fugue. Before he can intervene to regain control, he swings off into darkness and arrives instantaneously on a planet of purple sand and blue-leaved trees. Orange waves lap at the shore. He stands a few meters from a deep conical pit. Peering into it, he sees an amoebalike creature lying beside a human figure; strands of the alien's jellylike substance are wound around the man's body. He recognizes the man to be John Skein. The communion in the pit ends;

the man begins to clamber from the pit. The wind is rising. The sand, blown aloft, stains the sky grey. Patiently he watches his younger self struggling up from the pit. Now he understands. The circuit is closed; the knot is tied; the identity loop is complete. He is destined to spend many years on Abbondanza VI, growing ancient and withered. He is the skull-faced man.

Skein reaches the rim of the pit and lies there, breathing hard. He helps Skein get up.

"How do you feel?" he asks.

SCHWARTZ BETWEEN THE GALAXIES

This much is reality: Schwartz sits comfortably cocooned—passive, suspended—in a first-class passenger rack aboard a Japan Air Lines rocket, nine kilometers above the Coral Sea. And this much is fantasy: the same Schwartz has passage on a shining starship gliding silkily through the interstellar depths, en route at nine times the velocity of light from Betelgeuse IX to Rigel XXI, or maybe from Andromeda to the Lesser Magellanic.

There are no starships. Probably there never will be any. Here we are, a dozen decades after the flight of Apollo 11, and no human being goes anywhere except back and forth across the face of the little O, the Earth, for the planets are barren and the stars are beyond reach. That little O is too small for Schwartz. Too often it glazes for him; it turns to a nugget of dead porcelain; and lately he has formed the habit, when the world glazes, of taking refuge aboard that interstellar ship. So what JAL Flight 411 holds is merely his physical self, his shell, occupying a costly private cubicle on a slender 200-passenger vessel which, leaving Buenos Aires shortly after breakfast, has sliced westward along the Tropic of Capricorn for a couple of hours and will soon be landing at Papua's Torres Skyport. But his consciousness, his anima, the essential Schwartzness of him, soars between the galaxies.

What a starship it is! How marvelous its myriad passengers! Down its crowded corridors swarms a vast gaudy heterogeny of galactic creatures, natives of the worlds of Capella, Arcturus, Altair, Canopus, Polaris, Antares, beings both intelligent and articulate, methane-breathing or nitrogen-breathing or argon breathing, spiny-skinned or skinless, many-armed or many-headed or altogether incorporeal, each a product of a distinct and distinctly unique and alien cultural heritage. Among these varied folk moves Schwartz, that superstar of anthropologists, that true heir to Kroeber and Morgan and Malinowski and Mead, delightedly devouring their delicious diversity. Whereas aboard this prosaic rocket, this planet-locked stratosphere needle, one cannot tell the Canadians from the Portuguese, the Portuguese from the Romanians, the Romanians from the Irish, unless they open their mouths, and sometimes not always then.

In his reveries he confers with creatures from the Fomalhaut system about digital circumcision; he tapes the melodies of the Achernarnian eye-flute; he learns of the sneeze-magic of Acrux, the sleep-ecstasies of Aldebaran, the asteroid-sculptors of Thuban. Then a smiling JAL stewardess parts the curtain of his cubicle and peers in at him, jolting him from one reality to another. She is blue-eyed, frizzy-haired, straight-nosed, thin-lipped, bronze -skinned, a genetic mishmash, your standard twenty-first-century-model mongrel human, perhaps Melanesian-Swedish-Turkish- Bolivian, perhaps Polish-Berber-Tatar-Welsh. Cheap inter continental transit has done its deadly work: all Earth is a crucible, all the gene pools have melted into one indistinguishable fluid. Schwartz wonders about the recessivity of those blue eyes and arrives at no satisfactory solution. She is beautiful, at any rate. Her name is Dawn—O sweet neutral nonculture-bound cognomen!—and they have played at a flirtation, he and she, Dawn and Schwartz, at occasional moments of this short flight. Twinkling, she says softly, "We're getting ready for our landing, Dr. Schwartz. Are your restrictors in polarity?"

"I never unfastened them."

"Good." The blue eyes, warm, interested, meet his. "I have a layover in Papua tonight," she says.

"That's nice."

"Let's have a drink while we're waiting for them to unload the baggage," she suggests with cheerful bluntness. "All right?"

"I suppose," he says casually. "Why not?" Her availability bores him: somehow he enjoys the obsolete pleasures of the chase. Once such easiness in a woman like this would have excited him, but no longer. Schwartz is forty years old, tall, square-shouldered, sturdy, a showcase for the peasant genes of his rugged Irish mother. His close-cropped black hair is flecked with gray; many women find that interesting. One rarely sees gray hair now. He dresses simply but well, in sandals and Socratic tunic. Predictably, his physical attractiveness, both within his domestic sixness and without, has increased with his professional success. He is confident, sure of his powers, and he radiates an infectious assurance. This month alone eighty million people have heard his lectures.

She picks up the faint weariness in his voice. "You don't sound eager. Not interested?"

"Hardly that."

"What's wrong, then? Feeling sub, Professor?"

Schwartz shrugs. "Dreadfully sub. Body like dry bone. Mind like dead ashes." He smiles, full force depriving his words of all their weight.

She registers mock anguish. "That sounds bad," she says. "That sounds awful!"

"I'm only quoting Chuang Tzu. Pay no attention to me. Actually, I feel fine, just a little stale."

"Too many skyports?"

He nods. "Too much of a sameness wherever I go." He thinks of a star-bright, top-deck bubble dome where three boneless Spicans do a twining dance of propitiation to while away the slow hours of nine-light travel. "I'll be all right," he tells her. "It's a date."

Her hybrid face flows with relief and anticipation. "See you in Papua," she tells him, and winks, and moves jauntily down the aisle.

Papua. By cocktail time Schwartz will be in Port Moresby. Tonight he lectures at the University of Papua; yesterday it was Montevideo; the day after tomorrow it will be Bangkok. He is making the grand academic circuit. This is his year: he is very big, suddenly, in anthropological circles, since the publication of The Mask Beneath the Skin. From continent to continent he flashes, sharing his wisdom, Monday in Montreal, Tuesday Veracruz, Wednesday Montevideo, Thursday—Thursday? He crossed the international date line this morning, and he does not remember whether he has entered Thursday or Tuesday, though yesterday was surely Wednesday. Schwartz is certain only that this is July and the year is 2083, and there are moments when he is not even sure of that.

The JAL rocket enters the final phase of its landward plunge. Papua waits, sleek, vitrescent. The world has a glassy sheen again. He lets his spirit drift happily back to the gleaming starship making its swift way across the whirling constellations.

* * * *

He found himself in the starship's busy lower-deck lounge, having a drink with his traveling companion, Pitkin, the Yale economist. Why Pitkin, that coarse, florid little man? With all of real and imaginary humanity to choose from, why had his unconscious elected to make him share this fantasy with such a boor?

"Look," Pitkin said, winking and leering. "There's your girlfriend."

The entry-iris had opened and the Antarean not-male had come in.

"Quit it," Schwartz snapped. "You know there's no such thing going on."

"Haven't you been chasing her for days?"

"She's not a 'her'," Schwartz said.

Pitkin guffawed. "Such precision! Such scholarship! She's not a her, he says!" He gave Schwartz a broad nudge. "To you she's a she, friend, and don't try to kid me."

Schwartz had to admit there was some justice to Pitkin's vulgar innuendos. He did find the Antarean—a slim yellow-eyed ebony- skinned upright humanoid, sinuous and glossy, with tapering elongated limbs and a seal's fluid grace—powerfully attractive. Nor could he help thinking of the Antarean as feminine. That attitude was hopelessly culture-bound and species-bound, he knew; in fact the alien had cautioned him that terrestrial sexual distinctions were irrelevant in the Antares system, that if Schwartz insisted on thinking of "her" in genders, "she" could be considered only the negative of male, with no implication of biological femaleness.

He said patiently, "I've told you. The Antarean's neither male nor female as we understand those concepts. If we happen to perceive the Antarean as feminine, that's the result of our own cultural conditioning. If you want to believe that my interest in this being is sexual, go ahead, but I assure you that it's purely professional."

"Sure. You're only studying her."

"In a sense I am. And she's studying me. On her native world she has the status-frame of 'watcher-of-life,' which seems to translate into the Antarean equivalent of an anthropologist."

"How lovely for you both. She's your first alien and you're her first Jew."

"Stop calling her her," Schwartz hissed.

"But you've been doing it!"

Schwartz closed his eyes. "My grandmother told me never to get mixed up with economists. Their thinking is muddy and their breath is bad, she said. She also warned me against Yale men. Perverts of the intellect, she called them. So here I am cooped up on an interstellar ship with five hundred alien creatures and one fellow human, and he has to be an economist from Yale."

"Next trip travel with your grandmother instead."

"Go away," Schwartz said. "Stop lousing up my fantasies. Go peddle your dismal science somewhere else. You see those Delta Aurigans over there? Climb into their bottle and tell them all about the Gross Global Product." Schwartz smiled at the Antarean, who had purchased a drink, something that glittered an iridescent blue, and was approaching them. "Go on," Schwartz murmured.

"Don't worry," Pitkin said. "I wouldn't want to crowd you." He vanished into the motley crowd

The Antarean said, "The Capellans are dancing, Schwartz."

"I"d like to see that. Too damned noisy in here anyway." Schwartz stared into the alien's vertical-slitted citreous eyes. Cat's eyes, he thought. Panther's eyes. The Antarean's gaze was focused, as usual, on Schwartz's mouth: other worlds, other customs. He felt a strange, unsettling tremor of desire. Desire for what, though? It was a sensation of pure need, nonspecific, certainly nonsexual. "I think I'll take a look. Will you come with me?"

* * * *

The Papua rocket has landed. Schwartz, leaning across the narrow table in the skyport's lounge, says to the stewardess in a low, intense tone, "My life was in crisis. All my values were becoming meaningless. I was discovering that my chosen profession was empty, foolish, as useless as—playing chess."

"How awful," Dawn whispers gently.

"You can see why. You go all over the world, you see a thousand skyports a year. Everything the same everywhere. The same clothes, the same slang, the same magazines, the same styles of architecture and décor."

"Yes."

"International homogeneity. Worldwide uniformity. Can you understand what it's like to be an anthropologist in a world where there are no primitives left, Dawn? Here we sit on the island of Papua—you know, headhunters, animism, body-paint, the drums at sunset, the bone through the nose—and look at the Papuans in their business robes all around us. Listen to them exchanging stock-market tips, talking baseball, recommending restaurants in Paris and barbers in Johannesburg. It's no different anywhere else. In a single century we've transformed the planet into one huge sophisticated plastic western industrial state. The TV relay satellites, the two-hour intercontinental rockets, the breakdown of religious exclusivism and genetic taboo have mongrelized every culture, don't you see? You visit the Zuni and they have plastic African masks on the wall. You visit the Bushmen and they have Japanese-made Hopi-motif ashtrays. It's all just so much interior decoration, and underneath the carefully selected primitive motifs there's the same universal pseudo-American sensibility, whether you're in the Kalahari or the Amazon rain forest. Do you comprehend what's happened, Dawn?"

"It's such a terrible loss," she says sadly. She is trying very hard to be sympathetic, but he senses she is waiting for him to finish his sermon and invite her to share his hotel room. He will invite her, but there is no stopping him once he has launched into his one great theme.

"Cultural diversity is gone from the world," he says. "Religion is dead; true poetry is dead; inventiveness is dead; individuality is dead. Poetry. Listen to this." In a high monotone he chants:

* * * *

In beauty I walk
With beauty before me I walk
With beauty behind me I walk
With beauty above me I walk
With beauty above and about me I walk
It is finished in beauty
It is finished in beauty

* * * *

He has begun to perspire heavily. His chanting has created an odd sphere of silence in his immediate vicinity; heads are turning, eyes are squinting. "Navaho," he says. "The Night Way, a nine- day chant, a vision, a spell. Where are the Navaho now? Go to Arizona and they'll chant for you, yes, for a price, but they don't know what the words mean, and chances are the singers are only one-fourth Navaho, or one-eighth, or maybe just Hopi hired to dress in Navaho costumes, because the real Navaho, if any are left, are off in Mexico City hired to be Aztecs. So much is gone. Listen." He chants again, more piercingly even than before:

* * * *

The animal runs, it passes, it dies. And it is the great cold.
It is the great cold of the night, it is the dark.
The bird flies, it passes, it dies. And it is—

* * * *

"JAL FLIGHT 411 BAGGAGE IS NOW UNLOADING ON CONCOURSE FOUR," a mighty mechanical voice cries.

* * * *

—the great cold.
It is the great cold of the night, it is the dark.

* * * *

"JAL FLIGHT 411 BAGGAGE..."

* * * *

The fish flees, it passes, it dies. And—

* * * *

"People are staring," Dawn says uncomfortably.

"—ON CONCOURSE FOUR."

"Let them stare. Do them some good. That's a Pygmy chant, from Gabon, in equatorial Africa. Pygmies? There are no more Pygmies. Everybody's two meters tall. And what do we sing? Listen. Listen." He gestures fiercely at the cloud of tiny golden loudspeakers floating near the ceiling. A mush of music comes from them: the current popular favorite.

Savagely he mouths words: "Star...far...here...near. Playing in every skyport right now, all over the world." She smiles thinly. Her hand reaches toward his, covers it, presses against the knuckles. He is dizzy. The crowd, the eyes, the music, the drink. The plastic. Everything shines. Porcelain. Porcelain. The planet vitrifies. "Tom?" she asks uneasily. "Is anything the matter?" He laughs, blinks, coughs, shivers. He hears her calling for help, and then he feels his soul swooping outward, toward the galactic blackness.

* * * *

With the Antarean not-male beside him, Schwartz peered through the viewport, staring in awe and fascination at the seductive vision of the Capellans coiling and recoiling outside the ship. Not all the passengers on this voyage had cozy staterooms like his. The Capellans were too big to come on board, and in any case they preferred never to let themselves be enclosed inside metal walls. They traveled just alongside the starship, basking like slippery whales in the piquant radiations of space. So long as they kept within twenty meters of the hull they would be inside the effective field of the Rabinowitz Drive, which swept ship and contents and associated fellow travellers toward Rigel, or the Lesser Magellanic, or was it one of the Pleiades toward which they were bound at a cool nine lights?

He watched the Capellans moving beyond the shadow of the ship in tracks of shining white. Blue, glossy green, and velvet black, they coiled and swam, and every track was a flash of golden fire. "They have a dangerous beauty," Schwartz whispered. "Do you hear them calling? I do."

"What do they say?"

"They say, 'Come to me, come to me, come to me!'"

"Go to them, then," said the Antarean simply. "Step through the hatch."

"And perish?"

"And enter into your next transition. Poor Schwartz! Do you love your present body so?"

"My present body isn't so bad. Do you think I'm likely to get another one some day?"

"No?"

"No," Schwartz said. "This one is all I get. Isn't it that way with you?"

"At the Time of Openings I receive my next housing. That will be fifty years from now. What you see is the fifth form I have been given to wear."

"Will the next be as beautiful as this?"

"All forms are beautiful," the Antarean said. "You find me attractive?"

"Of course."

A slitted wink. A bobbing nod toward the viewport. "As attractive as those?"

Schwartz laughed. "Yes. In a different way."

Coquettishly the Antarean said, "If I were out there, you would walk through the hatch into space?"

"I might. If they gave me a spacesuit and taught me how to use it."

"But not otherwise? Suppose I were out there right now. I could live in space five, ten, maybe fifteen minutes. I am there and I say, 'Come to me, Schwartz, come to me!' What do you do?"

"I don't think I'm all that much self-destructive."

"To die for love, though! To make a transition for the sake of beauty."

"No. Sorry."

The Antarean pointed toward the undulating Capellans. "If they asked you, you would go."

"They are asking me," he said.

"And you refuse the invitation?"

"So far. So far."

The Antarean laughed an Antarean laugh, a thick silvery snort. "Our voyage will last many weeks more. One of these days, I think, you will go to them."

* * * *

"You were unconscious at least five minutes," Dawn says. "You gave everyone a scare. Are you sure you ought to go through with tonight's lecture?"

Nodding, Schwartz says, "I'll be all right. I'm a little tired, is all. Too many time zones this week." They stand on the terrace of his hotel room. Night is coming on, already, here in late afternoon: it is midwinter in the Southern Hemisphere, though the fragrance of tropic blossoms perfumes the air. The first few stars have appeared. He has never really known which star is which. That bright one, he thinks, could be Rigel, and that one Sirius, and perhaps this is Deneb over there. And this? Can this be red Antares, in the heart of the Scorpion, or is it only Mars? Because of his collapse at the skyport he has been able to beg off the customary faculty reception and the formal dinner; pleading the need for rest, he has arranged to have a simple snack at his hotel room, a deux. In two hours they will come for him and take him to the University to speak. Dawn watches him closely. Perhaps she is worried about his health, perhaps she is only waiting for him to make his move toward her. There's time for all that later, he figures. He would rather talk now. Warming up for the audience he seizes his earlier thread:

"For a long time I didn't understand what had taken place. I grew up insular, cut off from reality, a New York boy, bright mind and a library card. I read all the anthropological classics, Patterns of Culture and Coming of Age in Samoa and Life of a South African Tribe and the rest, and I dreamed of field trips, collecting myths and grammars and folkways and artefacts and all that, until when I was twenty-five I finally got out into the field and started to discover I had gone into a dead science. We have only one worldwide culture now, with local variants but no basic divergences—there's nothing primitive left on Earth, and there are no other planets. Not inhabited ones. I can't go to Mars or Venus or Saturn and study the natives. What natives? And we can't reach the stars. All I have to work with is Earth. I was thirty years old when the whole thing clicked together for me and I knew I had wasted my life."

She says, "But surely there was something for you to study on Earth."

"One culture, rootless and homogeneous. That's work for a sociologist, not for me. I'm a romantic, I'm an exotic, I want strangeness, difference. Look, we can never have any real perspective on our own time and lives. The sociologists try to attain it, but all they get is a mound of raw indigestible data. Insight comes later—two, five, ten generations later. But one way we've always been able to learn about ourselves is by studying alien cultures, studying them completely, and defining ourselves by measuring what they are that we aren't. The cultures have to be isolated, though. The anthropologist himself corrupts that isolation in the Heisenberg sense when he comes around with his camera and scanners and starts asking questions, but we can compensate more or less, for the inevitable damage a lone observer causes. We can't compensate when our whole culture collides with another and absorbs and obliterates it. Which we technological - mechanical people now have done everywhere. One day I woke up and saw there were no alien cultures left. Hah! Crushing revelation! Schwartz's occupation is gone!"

"What did you do?"

"For years I was in an absolute funk. I taught, I studied, I went through the motions, knowing it was all meaningless.

All I was doing was looking at records of vanished cultures left by earlier observers and trying to cudgel new meanings. Secondary sources, stale findings: I was an evaluator of dry bones, not a gatherer of evidence. Paleontology. Dinosaurs are interesting, but what do they tell you about the contemporary world and the meaning of its patterns? Dry bones, Dawn, dry bones. Despair. And then a clue. I had this Nigerian student, this Ibo—well, basically an Ibo, but she's got some Israeli in her and I think Chinese—and we grew very close, she was as close to me as anybody in my own sixness, and I told her my troubles. I'm going to give it all up, I said, because it isn't what I expected it to be. She laughed at me and said, What right do you have to be upset because the world doesn't live up to your expectations? Reshape your life, Tom; you can't reshape the world. I said, But how? And she said, Look inward, find the primitive in yourself, see what made you what you are, what made today's culture what it is, see how these alien streams have flowed together. Nothing's been lost here, only merged. Which made me think. Which gave me a new way of looking at things. Which sent me on an inward quest. It took me three years to grasp the patterns, to come to an understanding of what our planet has become, and only after I accepted the planet—"

It seems to him that he has been talking forever. Talking. Talking. But he can no longer hear his own voice. There is only a distant buzz.

"After I accepted—"

A distant buzz.

"What was I saying?" he asks.

"After you accepted the planet—"

"After I accepted the planet," he says, "that I could begin—" Buzz. Buzz. "That I could begin to accept myself."

* * * *

He was drawn toward the Spicans too, not so much for themselves—they were oblique, elliptical characters, self-contained and self-satisfied, hard to approach—as for the apparently psychedelic drug they took in some sacramental way before the beginning of each of their interminable ritual dances. Each time he had watched them take the drug, they had seemingly made a point of extending it toward him, as if inviting him, as if tempting him, before popping it into their mouths. He felt baited; he felt pulled.

There were three Spicans on board, slender creatures two and a half meters long, with flexible cylindrical bodies and small stubby limbs. Their skins were reptilian, dry and smooth, deep green with yellow bands, but their eyes were weirdly human, large liquid-brown eyes, sad Levantine eyes, the eyes of unfortunate medieval travelers transformed by enchantment into serpents. Schwartz had spoken with them several times. They understood English well enough—all galactic races did; Schwartz imagined it would become the interstellar lingua franca as it had on Earth—but the construction of their vocal organs was such that they had no way of speaking it, and they relied instead on small translating machines hung around their necks that converted their soft whispered hisses into amber words pulsing across a screen.

Cautiously, the third or fourth time he spoke with them, he expressed polite interest in their drug. They told him it enabled them to make contact with the central forces of the universe. He replied that there were such drugs on Earth, too, and that he used them frequently, that they gave him great insight into the workings of the cosmos. They showed some curiosity, perhaps even intense curiosity: reading their eyes was difficult and the tone of their voices gave no clues. He took his elegant leather-bound drug case from his pouch and showed them what he had: learitonin, psilocerebrin, siddharthin, and acid-57. He described the effects of each and suggested an exchange, any of his for an equivalent dose of the shriveled orange fungoid they nibbled. They conferred. Yes, they said, we will do this. But not now. Not until the proper moment. Schwartz knew better than to ask them when that would be. He thanked them and put his drugs away.

Pitkin, who had watched the interchange from the far side of the lounge, came striding fiercely toward him as the Spicans glided off. "What are you up to now?" he demanded.

"How about minding your own business?" Schwartz said amiably.

"You're trading pills with those snakes, aren't you?"

"Let's call it field research."

"Research? Research? What are you going to do, trip on that orange stuff of theirs?"

"I might," Schwartz said.

"How do you know what its effects on the human metabolism might be? You could end up blind or paralyzed or crazy or—"

"—or illuminated," Schwartz said. "Those are the risks one takes in the field. The early anthropologists who unhesitatingly sampled peyote and yage and ololiuqui accepted those risks, and—"

"But those were drugs that humans were using. You have no way of telling how—oh, what's the use, Schwartz? Research, he calls it. Research." Pitkin sneered. "Junkie!"

Schwartz matched him sneer for sneer. "Economist!"

* * * *

The house is a decent one tonight, close to three thousand, every seat in the University's great horseshoe-shaped auditorium taken, and a video relay besides, beaming his lecture to all Papua and half of Indonesia. Schwartz stands on the dais like a demigod under a brilliant no-glare spotlight. Despite his earlier weariness he is in good form now, gestures broad and forceful, eyes commanding, voice deep and resonant, words flowing freely. "Only one planet," he says, "one small and crowded planet, on which all cultures converge to a drab and depressing sameness. How sad that is! How tiny we make ourselves, when we make ourselves to resemble one another!" He flings his arms upward. "Look to the stars, the unattainable stars! Imagine, if you can, the millions of worlds that orbit those blazing suns beyond the night's darkness! Speculate with me on other peoples, other ways, other gods. Beings of every imaginable form, alien in appearance but not grotesque, not hideous, for all life is beautiful—beings that breathe gases strange to us, beings of immense size, beings of many limbs or of none, beings to whom death is a divine culmination of existence, beings who never die, beings who bring forth their young a thousand at a time, beings who do not reproduce—all the infinite possibilities of the infinite universe!

"Perhaps on each of those worlds it is as it has become here. One intelligent species, one culture, the eternal convergence. But the many worlds together offer a vast spectrum of variety. And now, share this vision with me! I see a ship voyaging from star to star, a spaceliner of the future, and aboard that ship is a sampling of many species, many cultures, a random scoop out of the galaxy's fantastic diversity. That ship is like a little cosmos, a small world, enclosed, sealed. How exciting to be aboard it, to encounter in that little compass such richness of cultural variation! Now our own world was once like that starship, a little cosmos, bearing with it all the thousands of Earthborn cultures. Hopi and Eskimo and Aztec and Kwakiutl and Arapesh and Orokolo and all the rest. In the course of our voyage we have come to resemble one another too much, and it has impoverished the lives of all of us, because—" He falters suddenly. He feels faint, and grasps the sides of the lectern. "Because—" The spotlight, he thinks. In my eyes. Not supposed to glare like that, but it's blinding. Got to have them move it. "In the course—the course of our voyage—" What's happening? Breaking into a sweat, now. Pain in my chest. My heart? Wait, slow up, catch your breath. That light in my eyes—

* * * *

"Tell me," Schwartz said earnestly, "what it's like to know you'll have ten successive bodies and live more than a thousand years."

"First tell me," said the Antarean, "what it's like to know you'll live ninety years or less and perish forever."

* * * *

Somehow he continues. The pain in his chest grows more intense, he cannot focus his eyes; he believes he will lose consciousness at any moment and may even have lost it already at least once, and yet he continues. Clinging to the lectern, he outlines the program he developed in The Mask Beneath the Skin. A rebirth of tribalism without a revival of ugly nationalism. The quest for a renewed sense of kinship with the past. A sharp reduction in nonessential travel, especially tourism. Heavy taxation of exported artefacts, including films and video shows. An attempt to create independent cultural units on Earth once again while maintain ing present levels of economic and political interdependence. Relinquishment of materialistic technological-industrial values. New searches for fundamental meanings. An ethnic revival, before it is too late, among those cultures of mankind that have only recently shed their traditional folkways. (He repeats and embellishes this point particularly, for the benefit of the Papuans before him, the great-grandchildren of cannibals.)

The discomfort and confusion come and go as he unreels his themes. He builds and builds, crying out passionately for an end to the homogenization of Earth, and gradually the physical symptoms leave him, all but a faint vertigo. But a different malaise seizes him as he nears his peroration. His voice becomes, to him, a far-off quacking, meaningless and foolish. He has said all this a thousand times, always to great ovations, but who listens? Who listens? Everything seems hollow tonight, mechanical, absurd. An ethnic revival? Shall these people before him revert to their loincloths and their pig roasts? His starship is a fantasy; his dream of a diverse Earth is mere silliness. What is, will be. And yet he pushes on toward his conclusion. He takes his audience back to that starship, he creates a horde of fanciful beings for them. He completes the metaphor by sketching the structures of half a dozen vanished "primitive" cultures of Earth, he chants the chants of the Navaho, the Gabon Pygmies, the Ashanti, the Mundugumor. It is over. Cascades of applause engulf him. He holds his place until members of the sponsoring committee come to him and help him down: they have perceived his distress. "It's nothing," he gasps. "The lights—

too bright—" Dawn is at his side. She hands him a drink, something cool. Two of the sponsors begin to speak of a reception for him in the Green Room. "Fine," Schwartz says. "Glad to." Dawn murmurs a protest. He shakes her off. "My obligation," he tells her. "Meet community leaders. Faculty people. I'm feeling better now. Honestly." Swaying, trembling, he lets them lead him away.

* * * *

"A Jew," the Antarean said. "You call yourself a Jew, but what is this exactly? A clan, a sept, a moiety, a tribe, a nation, what? Can you explain?"

"You understand what a religion is?"

"Of course."

"Judaism—Jewishness—it's one of Earth's major religions."

"You are therefore a priest?"

"Not at all. I don't even practice Judaism. But my ancestors did, and therefore I consider myself Jewish, even though—"

"It is an hereditary religion, then," the Antarean said, "that does not require its members to observe its rites?"

"In a sense," said Schwartz desperately. "More an hereditary cultural subgroup, actually, evolving out of a common religious outlook no longer relevant."

"Ah. And the cultural traits of Jewishness that define it and separate you from the majority of humankind are—?"

"Well—" Schwartz hesitated. "There's a complicated dietary code, a rite of circumcision for newborn males, a rite of passage for male adolescents, a language of scripture, a vernacular language that Jews all around the world more or less understand, and plenty more, including a certain intangible sense of clannishness and certain attitudes, such as a peculiar self-deprecating style of humor—"

"You observe the dietary code? You understand the language of scripture?"

"Not exactly," Schwartz admitted. "In fact I don't do anything that's specifically Jewish except think of myself as a Jew and adopt many of the characteristically Jewish personality modes, which however are not uniquely Jewish any longer—they can be traced among Italians, for example, and to some extent among Greeks. I'm speaking of Italians and Greeks of the late twentieth century, of course. Nowadays—" It was all becoming a terrible muddle. "Nowadays—"

"It would seem," said the Antarean, "that you are a Jew only because your maternal and paternal gene-givers were Jews, and they—"

"No, not quite. Not my mother, just my father, and he was Jewish only on his father's side, but even my grandfather never observed the customs, and—"

"I think this has grown too confusing," said the Antarean. "I withdraw the entire inquiry. Let us speak instead of my own traditions. The Time of Openings, for example, may be under stood as—"

* * * *

In the Green Room some eighty or a hundred distinguished Papuans press toward him, offering congratulations. "Absolutely right," they say. "A global catastrophe." "Our last chance to save our culture." Their skins are chocolate-tinted but their faces betray the genetic mishmash that is their ancestry: perhaps they call themselves Arapesh, Mundugumor, Tchambuli, Mafulu, in the way that he calls himself a Jew, but they have been liberally larded with chromosomes contributed by Chinese, Japanese, Europeans, Africans, everything. They dress in International Contemporary. They speak slangy, lively English. Schwartz feels seasick. "You look dazed," Dawn whispers. He smiles bravely. Body like dry bone. Mind like dead ashes. He is introduced to a tribal chieftain, tall, gray-haired, who looks and speaks like a professor, a lawyer, a banker. What, will these people return to the hills for the ceremony of the yam harvest? Will newborn girl-children be abandoned, cords uncut, skins unwashed, if their fathers do not need more girls? Will boys entering manhood submit to the expensive services of the initiator who scarifies them with the teeth of crocodiles? The crocodiles are gone. The shamans have become stockbrokers.

Suddenly he cannot breathe.

"Get me out of here," Schwartz mutters hoarsely, choking.

Dawn, with stewardess efficiency, chops a path for him through the mob. The sponsors, concerned, rush to his aid. He is floated swiftly back to the hotel in a glistening little bubble-car. Dawn helps him to bed. Reviving, he reaches for her.

"You don't have to," she says. "You've had a rough day."

He persists. He embraces her and takes her, quickly, fiercely, and they move together for a few minutes and it ends and he sinks back, exhausted, stupefied. She gets a cool cloth and pats his forehead and urges him to rest. "Bring me my drugs," he says. He wants siddharthin, but she misunderstands, probably deliberately, and offers him something blue and bulky, a sleeping pill, and, too weary to object, he takes it. Even so, it seems to be hours before sleep comes.

He dreams he is at the skyport, boarding the rocket for Bangkok, and instantly he is debarking at Bangkok—just like Port Moresby, only more humid—and he delivers his speech to a horde of enthusiastic Thais, while rockets flicker about him carrying him to skyport after skyport, and the Thais blur and become Japanese, who are transformed into Mongols, who become Uighurs, who become Iranians, who become Sudanese, who become Zambians, who become Chileans, and all look alike, all look alike, all look alike.

* * * *

The Spicans hovered above him, weaving, bobbing, swaying like cobras about to strike. But their eyes, warm and liquid, were sympathetic: loving, even. He felt the flow of their compassion. If they had had the sort of musculature that enabled them to smile, they would be smiling tenderly, he knew.

One of the aliens leaned close. The little translating device dangled toward Schwartz like a holy medallion. He narrowed his eyes, concentrating as intently as he could on the amber words flashing quickly across the screen.

"...has come. We shall..."

"Again, please," Schwartz said. "I missed some of what you were saying."

"The moment...has come. We shall...make the exchange of sacraments now."

"Sacraments?"

"Drugs."

"Drugs, yes. Yes. Of course." Schwartz groped in his pouch. He felt the cool, smooth leather skin of his drug case. Leather? Snakeskin, maybe. Anyway. He drew it forth. "Here," he said. "Siddharthin, learitonin, psilocerebrin, acid-57. Take your pick." The Spicans selected three small blue siddharthins. "Very good," Schwartz said. "The most transcendental of all. And now—"

The longest of the aliens proffered a ball of dried orange fungus the size of Schwartz's thumbnail.

"It is an equivalent dose. We give it to you."

"Equivalent to all three of my tablets, or to one?"

"Equivalent. It will give you peace."

Schwartz smiled. There was a time for asking questions and a time for unhesitating action. He took the fungus and reached for a glass of water.

"Wait!" Pitkin cried, appearing suddenly. "What are you—"

"Too late," Schwartz said serenely, and swallowed the Spican drug in one joyous gulp.

* * * *

The nightmares go on and on. He circles the Earth like the Flying Dutchman, like the Wandering Jew, skyport to skyport to skyport, an unending voyage from nowhere to nowhere. Obliging com mittees meet him and convey him to his hotel. Sometimes the committee members are contemporary types, indistinguishable from one another, with standard faces, standard clothing, the all- purpose new-model hybrid unihuman, and sometimes they are consciously ethnic, elaborately decked out in feathers and paint and tribal emblems, but their faces, too, are standard behind the gaudy regalia, their slang is the slang of Uganda and Tierra del Fuego and Nepal, and it seems to Schwartz that these masqueraders are, if anything, less authentic, less honest, than the other sort, who at least are true representatives of their era. So it is hopeless either way. He lashes at his pillow, he groans, he wakens. Instantly Dawn's arms enfold him. He sobs incoherent phrases into her clavicle and she murmurs soothing sounds against his forehead. He is having some sort of breakdown, he realizes: a new crisis of values, a shattering of the philosophical synthesis that has allowed him to get through the last few years. He is bound to the wheel; he spins, he spins, he spins, traversing the continents, getting nowhere. There is no place to go. No. There is one, just one, a place where he will find peace, where the universe will be as he needs it to be. Go there, Schwartz. Go and stay as long as you can. "Is there anything I can do?" Dawn asks. He shivers and shakes his head. "Take this," she says, and gives him some sort of pill. Another tranquilizer. All right. All right. The world has turned to porcelain. His skin feels like a plastic coating. Away, away, to the ship. To the ship! "So long," Schwartz says.

* * * *

Outside the ship the Capellans twist and spin in their ritual dance as, weightless and without mass, they are swept toward the rim of the galaxy at nine times the velocity of light. They move with a grace that is astonishing for creatures of such tremendous bulk. A dazzling light that emanates from the center of the universe strikes their glossy skin and, rebounding, resonates all up and down the spectrum, splintering into brilliant streamers of ultra red, infraviolet, exoyellow. All the cosmos glows and shimmers. A single perfect note of music comes out of the remote distance and, growing closer, swells in an infinite crescendo. Schwartz trembles at the beauty of all he perceives.

Beside him stands the seal-slick Antarean. She—definitely she, no doubt of it, she—plucks at his arm and whispers, "Will you go to them?"

"Yes. Yes, of course."

"So will I. Wherever you go."

"Now," Schwartz says. He reaches for the lever that opens the hatch. He pulls down. The side of the starship swings open.

The Antarean looks deep into his eyes and says blissfully, "I never told you my name. My name is Dawn."

Together they float through the hatch into space.

The blackness receives them gently. There is no chill, no pressure at the lungs, no discomfort at all. He is surrounded by luminous surges, by throbbing mantles of pure color, as though he has entered the heart of an aurora. He and Dawn swim toward the Capellans, and the huge beings welcome them with deep, glad, booming cries. Dawn joins the dance at once, moving her sinuous limbs with extravagant ease; Schwartz will do the same in a moment, but first he turns to face the starship, hanging in space close by him like a vast coppery needle, and in a voice that could shake universes he calls, "Come, friends! Come, all of you! Come dance with us!" And they come, pouring through the hatch, the Spicans first, then all the rest, the infinite multitude of beings, the travelers from Fomalhaut and Achernar and Acrux and Aldebaran, from Thuban and Arcturus and Altair, from Polaris and Canopus and Sirius and Rigel, hundreds of star-creatures spilling happily out of the vessel, bursting forth, all of them, even Pitkin, poor little Pitkin, everyone joining hands and tentacles and tendrils and whatever, forming a great ring of light across space, everyone locked in a cosmic harmony, everyone dancing. Dancing. Dancing.

GIANNI

"But why not Mozart?" Hoaglund said, shaking his head. "Schubert, even? Or you could have brought back Bix Beiderbecke, for Christ's sake, if you wanted to resurrect a great musician."

"Beiderbecke was jazz," I said. "I'm not interested in jazz. Nobody's interested in jazz except you."

"And people are still interested in Pergolesi in the year 2008?"

"I am."

"Mozart would have been better publicity. You'll need more funding sooner or later. You tell the world you've got Mozart sitting in the back room cranking out a new opera, you can write your own ticket. But what good is Pergolesi? Pergolesi's totally forgotten."

"Only by the proletariat, Sam. Besides, why give Mozart a second chance? Maybe he died young, but it wasn't all that young, and he did his work, a ton of work. Gianni died at twenty-six, you know. He might have been greater than Mozart if he'd had another dozen years."

"Johnny?"

"Gianni. Giovanni Battista. Pergolesi. He calls himself Gianni. Come meet him."

"Mozart, Dave. You should have done Mozart."

"Stop being an idiot," I said. "When you've met him, you'll know I did the right thing. Mozart would have been a pain in the neck, anyway. The stories I've heard about Mozart's private life would uncurl your wig. Come on with me."

I led him down the long hallway from the office past the hardware room and the timescoop cage to the airlock separating us from the semidetached motel unit out back where Gianni had been living since we scooped him. We halted in the airlock to be sprayed. Sam frowned and I explained, "Infectious microorganisms have mutated a lot since the eighteenth century. Until we've got his resistance levels higher, we're keeping him in a pretty sterile environment. When we first brought him back, he was vulnerable to anything—a case of the sniffles would have killed him, most likely. Plus he was a dying man when we got him, one lung lousy with TB and the other one going."

"Hey," Hoaglund said.

I laughed. “You won’t catch anything from him. It’s in remission now, Sam. We didn’t bring him back at colossal expense just to watch him die.”

The lock opened and we stepped into the monitoring vestibule, glittering like a movie set with bank upon bank of telemetering instruments. The day nurse, Claudia, was checking diagnostic readouts. “He’s expecting you, Dr. Leavis,” she said. “He’s very frisky this morning.”

“Frisky?”

“Playful. You know.”

Yes. Tacked to the door of Gianni’s room was a card that hadn’t been there yesterday, flamboyantly lettered in gaudy, free-flowing baroque script:

* * * *

GIOVANNI BATTISTA PERGOLESI

Jesi, January 3 1710—Pozzuoli, March 17 1736

Los Angeles, Dec. 20 2007—.

Genuis At Work!!!!

Per Piacere, Knock Before You enter!

* * * *

“He speaks English?” Hoaglund asked.

“Now he does,” I said. “We gave him tapesleep the first week. He picks things up fast, anyway.” I grinned. “Genius at work, eh? Or genuis. That’s the sort of sign I would have expected Mozart to put up.”

“They’re all alike, these talents,” Hoaglund said.

I knocked.

"Chi va là?" Gianni called.

"Dave Leavis."

"Avanti, dottore illustrissimo!"

"I thought you said he speaks English," Hoaglund murmured.

"He's frisky today, Claudia said, remember?"

We went in. As usual he had the blinds tightly drawn, shutting out the brilliant January sunlight, the yellow blaze of acacia blossoms just outside the window, the enormous scarlet bougainvillea, the sweeping hilltop vista of the valley and the mountains beyond. Maybe scenery didn't interest him—or, more likely, he preferred to keep his room a tightly sealed little cell, an island out of time. He had had to absorb a lot of psychic trauma in the past few weeks: it must give you a hell of a case of jet-lag to jump 271 years into the future.

But he looked lively, almost impish—a small man, graceful, delicate, with sharp, busy eyes, quick, elegant gestures, a brisk, confident manner. How much he had changed in just a few weeks! When we fished him out of the eighteenth century, he was a woeful sight, face lined and haggard, hair already gray at twenty-six, body gaunt, bowed, quivering. He looked like what he was, a shattered consumptive a couple of weeks from the grave. His hair was still gray, but he had gained ten pounds; the veils were gone from his eyes; there was color in his cheeks.

I said, "Gianni, I want you to meet Sam Hoaglund. He's going to handle publicity and promotion for our project. Capisce? He will make you known to the world and give you a new audience for your music."

He flashed a brilliant smile. "Bene. Listen to this."

The room was an electronic jungle, festooned with gadgetry: a synthesizer, a telescreen, a megabuck audio library, five sorts of data terminals and all manner of other things perfectly suited to your basic eighteenth-century Italian drawing room. Gianni loved it all and was mastering the equipment with astonishing, even frightening, ease. He swung around to the synthesizer, jacked it into harpsichord mode and touched the keyboard. From the cloud of floating minispeakers came the opening theme of a sonata, lovely, lyrical, to my ear unmistakably Pergolesian in its melodiousness, and yet somehow weird. For all its beauty there was a strained, awkward, suspended aspect to it, like a ballet performed by dancers in galoshes. The longer he played, the more uncomfortable I felt. Finally he turned to us and said, "You like it?"

"What is it? Something of yours?"

"Mine, yes. My new style. I am under the influence of Beethoven today. Haydn yesterday, tomorrow Chopin. I try everything, no? By Easter I get to the ugly composers. Mahler, Berg, Debussy—those men were crazy, do you know? Crazy music, so ugly. But I will learn."

"Debussy ugly?" Hoaglund said quietly to me.

"Bach is modern music to him," I said. "Haydn is the voice of the future."

Gianni said, "I will be very famous."

"Yes. Sam will make you the most famous man in the world."

"I was very famous after I—died." He tapped one of the terminals. "I have read about me. I was so famous that everybody forged my music, and it was published as Pergolesi, do you know that? I have played it, too, this 'Pergolesi.' Merda, most of it. Not all. The concerti armonici, not bad—not mine, but not bad. Most of the rest, trash." He winked. "But you will make me famous while I live, eh? Good. Very good." He came closer to us and in a lower voice said, "Will you tell Claudia that the gonorrhea, it is all cured?"

"What?"

"She would not believe me. I said, The doctor swears it, but she said, "No, it is not safe; you must keep your hands off me; you must keep everything else off me."

"Gianni, have you been molesting your nurse?"

"I am becoming a healthy man, dottore. I am no monk. They sent me to live with the cappuccini in the monastery at Pozzuoli, yes, but it was only so the good air there could heal my consumption, not to make me a monk. I am no monk now and I am no longer sick. Could you go without a woman for three hundred years?" He put his face close to Hoaglund's, gave him a bright-eyed stare, leered outrageously. "You will make me very famous. And then there will be women again, yes? And you must tell them that the gonorrhea, it is entirely cured. This age of miracles!"

Afterward Hoaglund said to me, "And you thought Mozart was going to be too much trouble?"

* * * *

When we first got him, there was no snappy talk out of him of women or fame or marvelous new compositions. Then he was a wreck, a dazed wraith, hollow, burned out. He wasn't sure whether he had awakened in heaven or in hell, but whichever it was left him alternately stunned and depressed. He was barely clinging to life, and we began to wonder if we had waited too long to get him. Perhaps it might be wiser, some of us thought, to toss him back and pick him up from an earlier point, maybe summer of 1735, when he wasn't so close to the grave. But we had no budget for making a second scoop, and also we were bound by our own rigid self-imposed rules. We had the power to yank anybody we liked out of the past—Napoleon, Genghis Khan, Jesus, Henry the Eighth—but we had no way of knowing what effects it might have on the course of history if we scooped up Lenin while he was still in exile in Switzerland, say, or collected Hitler while he was still a paperhanger. So we decided a priori to scoop only someone whose life and accomplishments were entirely behind him, and who was so close to the time of his natural death that his disappearance would not be likely to unsettle the fabric of the universe. For months I lobbied to scoop Pergolesi, and I got my way, and we took him out of the monastery eighteen days before his official date of death. Once we had him, it was no great trick to substitute a synthetic cadaver, who was duly discovered and buried, and so far as we have been able to tell, no calamities have resulted to history because one consumptive Italian was put in his grave two weeks earlier than the encyclopedia used to say he had been.

Yet it was touch and go at first, keeping him alive. Those were the worst days of my life, the first few after the scooping. To have planned for years, to have expended so many gigabucks on the project, and then to have our first human scoopee die on us anyway—

He didn't, though. The same vitality that had pulled sixteen operas and a dozen cantatas and uncountable symphonies and concerti and masses and sonatas out of him in a twenty-six-year lifespan pulled him back from the edge of the grave now, once the resources of modern medicine were put to work rebuilding his lungs and curing his assorted venereal diseases. From hour to hour we could see him gaining strength. Within days he was wholly transformed. It was almost magical, even to us. And it showed us vividly how many lives were needlessly lost in those archaic days for want of the things that are routine to us antibiotics, transplant technology, micro-surgery, regeneration therapy.

For me those were wondrous days. The pallid, feeble young man struggling for his life in the back unit was surrounded by a radiant aura of accumulated fame and legend built up over centuries: he was Pergolesi, the miraculous boy, the fountain of melody, the composer of the awesome Stabat Mater and the rollicking Serva Padrona, who in the decades after his early death was ranked with Bach, with Mozart, with Haydn, and whose most trivial works inspired the whole genre of light opera. But his own view of himself was different: he was a weary, sick, dying young man, poor pathetic Gianni, the failure, the washout, unknown beyond Rome and Naples and poorly treated there, his serious operas neglected cruelly, his masses and cantatas praised but rarely performed, only the comic operas that he dashed off so carelessly winning him any acclaim at all—poor Gianni, burned out at twenty-five, destroyed as much by disappointment as by tuberculosis and venereal disease, creeping off to the Capuchin monastery to die in miserable poverty. How could he have known he was to be famous? But we showed him. We played him recordings of his music, both the true works and those that had been constructed in his name by the unscrupulous to cash in on his posthumous glory. We let him read the biographies and critical studies and even the novels that had been published about him. Indeed, for him it must have been precisely like dying and going to heaven, and from day to day he gained strength and poise, he waxed and flourished, he came to glow with vigor and passion and confidence. He knew now that no magic had been worked on him, that he had been snatched into the unimaginable future and restored to health by ordinary human beings, and he accepted that and quickly ceased to question it. All that concerned him now was music. In the second and third weeks we gave him a crash course in post-Baroque musical history. Bach first, then the shift away from polyphony—"Naturalmente," he said, "it was inevitable, I would have achieved it myself if I had lived"—and he spent hours with Mozart and Haydn and Johann Christian Bach, soaking up their complete works and entering a kind of ecstatic state. His nimble, agile mind swiftly began plotting its own directions. One morning I found him red-eyed with weeping. He had been up all night listening to Don Giovanni and Marriage of Figaro. "This Mozart," he said. "You bring him back, too?"

"Maybe someday we will," I said.

"I kill him! You bring him back, I strangle him, I trample him!" His eyes blazed. He laughed wildly. "He is wonder! He is angel! He is too good! Send me to his time, I kill him then! No one should compose like that! Except Pergolesi. He would have done it."

"I believe that."

"Yes! This Figaro—1786—I could have done it twenty years earlier! Thirty! If only I get the chance. Why this Mozart so lucky? I die, he live—why? Why, dottore?"

His love-hate relationship with Mozart lasted six or seven days. Then he moved on to Beethoven, who I think was a little too much for him, overwhelming, massive, crushing, and then the romantics, who amused him—"Berlioz, Tchaikovsky, Wagner, all lunatics, dementi, pazzi, but they are wonderful. I think I see what they are trying to do. Madmen! Marvelous madmen!"and quickly on to the twentieth century, Mahler, Schoenberg, Stravinsky, Bartok, not spending much time with any of them, finding them all either ugly or terrifying or simply incomprehensibly bizarre. More recent composers, Webern and the serialists, Penderecki, Stockhausen, Xenakis, Ligeti, the various electronicists and all that came after, he dismissed with a quick shrug, as though he barely recognized what they were doing as music. Their fundamental assumptions were too alien to him. Genius though he was, he could not assimilate their ideas, any more than Brillat-Savarin or Escoffier could have found much pleasure in the cuisine of another planet. After completing his frenzied survey of everything that had happened in music after his time, he returned to Bach and Mozart and gave them his full attention.

I mean full attention. Gianni was utterly incurious about the world outside his bedroom window. We told him he was in America, in California, and showed him a map. He nodded casually. We turned on the telescreen and let him look at the landscape of the early twenty-first century. His eyes glazed. We spoke of automobiles, planes, flights to Mars. Yes, he said, meraviglioso, miracoloso, and went back to the Brandenburg concerti. I realize now that the lack of interest he showed in the modern world was a sign neither of fear nor of shallowness, but rather only a mark of priorities. What Mozart had accomplished was stranger and more interesting to him than the entire technological revolution. Technology was only a means to an end, for Gianni—push a button, you get a symphony orchestra in your bedroom: miracoloso!—and he took it entirely for granted. That the basso continuo had become obsolete thirty years after his death, that the diatonic scales would be demoted from sacred constants to inconvenient anachronisms a century or so later, was more significant to him than the fusion reactor, the interplanetary spaceship, or even the machine that had yanked him from his deathbed into this brave new world.

In the fourth week he said he wanted to compose again. He asked for a harpsichord. Instead we gave him a synthesizer. He loved it.

In the sixth week he began asking questions about the outside world, and I realized that the tricky part of our experiment was about to begin.

* * * *

Hoaglund said, "Pretty soon we have to reveal him. It's incredible we've been able to keep it quiet this long."

He had an elaborate plan. The problem was twofold: letting Gianni experience the world, and letting the world perceive that time-travel as a practical matter involving real human beings—no more frogs and kittens hoisted from last month to this—had finally arrived. There was going to be a whole business of press conferences, media tours of our lab, interviews with Gianni, a festival of Pergolesi music at the Hollywood Bowl with the premiere of a symphony in the mode of Beethoven that he said would be ready by April, et cetera, et cetera, et cetera. But at the same time we would be taking Gianni on private tours of the L.A. area, gradually exposing him to the society into which he had been so unilaterally hauled. The medics said it was safe to let him encounter twenty-first-century microorganisms now. But would it be safe to let him encounter twenty-first-century civilization? He, with his windows sealed and his blinds drawn, his eighteenth-century mind wholly engrossed in the revelations that Bach and Mozart and Beethoven were pouring into it—what would he make of the world of spaceways and slice-houses and overload bands and freebase teams when he could no longer hide from it?

"Leave it all to me," said Hoaglund. "That's what you're paying me for, right?"

On a mild and rainy February afternoon Sam and I and the main physician, Nella Brandon, took him on his first drive through his new reality. Down the hill the back way, along Ventura Boulevard a few miles, onto the freeway, out to Topanga, back around through the landslide zone to what had been Santa Monica, and then straight up Wilshire across the entire heart of Los Angeles—a good stiff jolt of modernity. Dr. Brandon carried her full armamentarium of sedatives and tranks ready in case Gianni freaked out. But he didn't freak out.

He loved it—swinging round and round in the bubbletop car, gaping at everything. I tried to view L.A. through the eyes of someone whose entire life had been spent amid the splendors of Renaissance and Baroque architecture, and it came up hideous on all counts. But not to Gianni. "Beautiful," he sighed. "Wondrous! Miraculous! Marvelous!" The traffic, the freeways themselves, the fast-food joints, the peeling plastic facades, the great fire scar in Topanga, the houses hanging by spider-cables from the hillsides, the occasional superjet floating overhead on its way into LAX—everything lit him up. It was wonderland to him. None of those dull old cathedrals and palazzi and marble fountains here—no, everything here was brighter and larger and glitzier than life, and he loved it. The only part he couldn't handle was the beach at Topanga. By the time we got there the sun was out and so were the sunbathers, and the sight of eight thousand naked bodies cavorting on the damp sand almost gave him a stroke."What is this?" he demanded. "The market for slaves? The pleasure house of the king?"

"Blood pressure rising fast," Nella Brandon said softly, eyeing her wrist-monitors. "Adrenalin levels going up. Shall I cool him out?"

I shook my head.

"Slavery is unlawful," I told him. "There is no king. These are ordinary citizens amusing themselves."

"Nudo! Assolutamente nudo!"

"We long ago outgrew feeling ashamed of our bodies," I said. "The laws allow us to go nude in places like this."

"Straordinario! Incredibile!" He gaped in total astonishment. Then he erupted with questions, a torrent of Italian first, his English returning only with an effort. Did husbands allow their wives to come here? Did fathers permit daughters? Were there rapes on the beach? Duels? If the body had lost its mystery, how did sexual desire survive? If a man somehow did become excited, was it shameful to let it show? And on and on and on, until I had to signal Nella to give him a mild needle. Calmer now, Gianni digested the notion of mass public nudity in a more reflective way; but it had amazed him more than Beethoven, that was plain.

We let him stare for another ten minutes. As we started to return to the car, Gianni pointed to a lush brunette trudging along by the tide-pools and said, "I want her. Get her."

"Gianni, we can't do that!"

"You think I am eunuch? You think I can see these bodies and not remember breasts in my hands, tongue touching tongue?" He caught my wrist. "Get her for me."

"Not yet. You aren't well enough yet. And we can't just get her for you. Things aren't done that way here."

"She goes naked. She belongs to anyone."

"No," I said. "You still don't really understand, do you?" I nodded to Nella Brandon. She gave him another needle. We drove on, and he subsided. Soon we came to the barrier marking where the coast road had fallen into the sea, and we swung inland through the place where Santa Monica had been. I explained about the earthquake and the landslide. Gianni grinned.

"Ah, il terremoto, you have it here too? A few years ago there was great earthquake in Napoli. You have understood? And then they ask me to write a Mass of Thanksgiving afterward because not everything is destroyed. It is very famous mass for a time. You know it? No? You must hear it." He turned and seized my wrist. With an intensity greater than the brunette had aroused in him, he said, "I will compose a new famous mass, yes? I will be very famous again. And I will be rich. Yes? I was famous and then I was forgotten and then I died and now I live again and now I will be famous again. And rich. Yes? Yes?"

Sam Hoaglund looked over at him and said, "In another couple of weeks, Gianni, you're going to be the most famous man in the world."

Casually Sam poked the button turning on the radio. The car was well equipped for overload and out of the many speakers came the familiar pulsing tingling sounds of Wilkes Booth John doing Membrane. The subsonics were terrific. Gianni sat up straight as the music hit him. "What is that?" he demanded.

"Overload," Sam said. "Wilkes Booth John."

"Overload? This means nothing to me. It is a music? Of when?"

"The music of right now," said Nella Brandon.

As we zoomed along Wilshire Sam keyed in the colors and lights too, and the whole interior of the car began to throb and flash and sizzle. Wonderland for Gianni again. He blinked, he pressed his hands to his cheeks, he shook his head. “It is like the music of dreams,” he said. “The composer? Who is?”

“Not a composer,” said Sam. “A group. Wilkes Booth John, it calls itself. This isn’t classical music, it’s pop. Popular. Pop doesn’t have a composer.”

“It makes itself, this music?”

“No,” I said. “The whole group composes it. And plays it.”

“The orchestra. It is pop and the orchestra composes.” He looked lost, as bewildered as he had been since the moment of his awakening, naked and frail, in the scoop cage. “Pop. Such strange music. So simple. It goes over and over again, the same thing, loud, no shape. Yet I think I like it. Who listens to this music? Imbecili? Infanti?”

“Everyone,” Sam said.

* * * *

The first outing in Los Angeles not only told us Gianni could handle exposure to the modern world but also transformed his life among us in several significant ways. For one thing, there was no keeping him chaste any longer after Topanga Beach. He was healthy, he was lusty, he was vigorously heterosexual—an old biography of him I had seen blamed his ill health and early demise on “his notorious profligacy”—and we could hardly go on treating him like a prisoner or a zoo animal. Sam fixed him up with one of his secretaries, Melissa Burke, a willing volunteer.

Then, too, Gianni had been confronted for the first time with the split between classical and popular music, with the whole modernist cleavage between high art and lowbrow entertainment. That was new to him and baffling at first. "This pop," he said, "it is the music of the peasants?" But gradually he grasped the idea of simple rhythmic music that everyone listened to, distinguished from "serious" music that belonged only to an elite and was played merely on formal occasions. "But my music," he protested, "it had tunes, people could whistle it. It was everybody's music." It fascinated him that composers had abandoned melody and made themselves inaccessible to most of the people. We told him that something like that had happened in all of the arts. "You poor crazy futuruomini," he said gently.

Suddenly he began to turn himself into a connoisseur of overload groups. We rigged an imposing unit in his room, and he and Melissa spent hours plugged in, soaking up the waveforms let loose by Scissors and Ultrafoam and Wilkes Booth John and the other top bands. When I asked him how the new symphony was coming along, he gave me a peculiar look.

He began to make other little inroads into modern life. Sam and Melissa took him shopping for clothing on Figueroa Street, and in the cholo boutiques he acquired a flashy new wardrobe of the latest Aztec gear to replace the lab clothes he had worn since his awakening. He had his prematurely gray hair dyed red. He acquired jewelry that went flash, clang, zzz, and pop when the mood-actuated sensoria came into play. In a few days he was utterly transformed: he became the perfect young Angeleno, slim, dapper, stylish, complete with the slight foreign accent and exotic grammar.

"Tonight Melissa and I go to The Quonch," Gianni announced.

"The Quonch," I murmured, mystified.

"Overload palace," Hoaglund explained. "In Pomona. All the big groups play there."

"We have Philharmonic tickets tonight," I said feebly.

Gianni's eyes were implacable. "The Quonch," he said.

So we went to The Quonch. Gianni, Melissa, Sam, Sam's slice-junkie livewith, Oreo, and I. Gianni and Melissa had wanted to go alone, but I wasn't having that. I felt a little like an overprotective mother whose little boy wanted to try a bit of freebasing. No chaperones, no Quonch, I said. The Quonch was a gigantic geodesic dome in Pomona Downlevel, far underground. The stage whirled on antigrav gyros, the ceiling was a mist of floating speakers, the seats had pluggie intensifiers, and the audience, median age about fourteen, was sliced out of its mind. The groups performing that night were Thug, Holy Ghosts, Shining Orgasm Revival and Ultrafoam. For this I had spent untold multi-kilogelt to bring the composer of the Stabat Mater and La Serva Padrona back to life? The kids screamed, the great hall filled with dense, tangible, oppressive sound, colors and lights throbbed and pulsed, minds were blown. In the midst of the madness sat Giovanni Battista Pergolesi (1710–1736), graduate of the Conservatorio dei Poveri, organist of the royal chapel at Naples, maestro di capella to the Prince of Stigliano—plugged in, turned on, radiant, ecstatic, transcendent.

Whatever else The Quonch may have been, it didn't seem dangerous, so the next night I let Gianni go there just with Melissa. And the next. It was healthy for both of us to let him move out on his own a little. But I was starting to worry. It wouldn't be long until we broke the news to the public that we had a genuine eighteenth-century genius among us. But where were the new symphonies? Where were the heaven-sent sonatas? He wasn't producing anything visible. He was just doing a lot of overload. I hadn't brought him back here to be a member of the audience, especially that audience.

"Relax," Sam Hoaglund said. "He's going through a phase. He's dazzled by the novelty of everything, and also he's having fun for maybe the first time in his life. But sooner or later he'll get back to composing. Nobody steps out of character forever. The real Pergolesi will take control."

Then Gianni disappeared.

Came the frantic call at three in the afternoon on a crazy hot Saturday with Santa Anas blowing and a fire raging in Tujunga. Dr. Brandon had gone to Gianni's room to give him his regular checkup, and no Gianni. I went whistling across town from my house near the beach. Hoaglund, who had come running in from Santa Barbara, was there already. "I phoned Melissa," he said. "He's not with her. But she's got a theory."

"Tell."

"They've been going backstage the last few nights. He's met some of the kids from Ultrafoam and one of the other groups. She figures he's off jamming with them."

"If that's all, then hallelujah. But how do we track him?"

"She's getting addresses. We're making calls. Quit worrying, Dave."

Easy to say. I imagined him held for ransom in some East L.A. dive. I imagined swaggering machos sending me his fingers, one a day, waiting for fifty megabucks' payoff. I paced for half a dreadful hour, grabbing up phones as if they were magic wands, and then came word that they had found him working out with Shining Orgasm Revival in a studio in West Covina. We were there in half the legal time and to hell with the California Highway Patrol.

The place was a miniature Quonch, electronic gear everywhere, the special apparatus of overload rigged up, and Gianni sitting in the midst of six practically naked young uglies whose bodies were draped with readout tape and sonic gadgetry. So was his. He looked blissful and sweaty. "It is so beautiful, this music," he sighed when I collared him. "It is the music of my second birth. I love it beyond everything."

"Bach," I said. "Beethoven. Mozart."

"This is other. This is miracle. The total effect—the surround, the engulf—"

"Gianni, don't ever go off again without telling someone."

"You were afraid?"

"We have a major investment in you. We don't want you getting hurt or into trouble or—"

"Am I a child?"

"There are dangers in this city that you couldn't possibly understand yet. You want to jam with these musicians, jam with them, but don't just disappear. Understood?"

He nodded.

Then he said, "We will not hold the press conference for a while. I am learning this music. I will make my debut next month, maybe. If we can get booking at The Quonch as main attraction."

"This is what you want to be? An overload star?"

"Music is music."

"And you are Giovanni Battista Pergo—" An awful thought struck me. I looked sidewise at Shining Orgasm Revival. "Gianni, you didn't tell them who you—"

"No. I am still secret."

"Thank God." I put my hand on his arm. "Look, if this stuff amuses you, listen to it, play it, do what you want. But the Lord gave you a genius for real music."

"This is real music."

"Complex music. Serious music."

"I starved to death composing that music."

"You were ahead of your time. You wouldn't starve now. You will have a tremendous audience for your music."

"Because I am a freak, yes. And in two months I am forgotten again. Grazie, no, Dave. No more sonatas. No more cantatas. Is not the music of this world. I give myself to overload."

"I forbid it, Gianni!"

He glared. I saw something steely behind his delicate and foppish exterior.

"You do not own me, Dr. Leavis."

"I gave you life."

"So did my father and mother. They didn't own me either."

"Please, Gianni. Let's not fight. I'm only begging you not to turn your back on your genius, not to renounce the gift God gave you for—"

"I renounce nothing. I merely transform." He leaned up and put his nose almost against mine. "Let me free. I will not be a court composer for you. I will not give you masses and symphonies. No one wants such things today, not new ones, only a few people who want the old ones. Not good enough. I want to be famous, capisce? I want to be rich. Did you think I'd live the rest of my life as a curiosity, a museum piece? Or that I would learn to write the kind of noise they call modern music? Fame is what I want. I died poor and hungry, the books say. You die poor and hungry and find out what it is like, and then talk to me about writing cantatas. I will never be poor again." He laughed. "Next year, after I am revealed to the world, I will start my own overload group. We will wear wigs, eighteenth-century clothes, everything. We will call ourselves Pergolesi. All right? All right, Dave?"

He insisted on working out with Shining Orgasm Revival every afternoon. Okay. He went to overload concerts just about every night. Okay. He talked about going on stage next month. Even that was okay. He did no composing, stopped listening to any music but overload. Okay. He is going through a phase, Sam Hoaglund had said. Okay. You do not own me, Gianni had said.

Okay. Okay.

I let him have his way. I asked him who his overload playmates thought he was, why they had let him join the group so readily. "I say I am rich Italian playboy," he replied. "I give them the old charm, you understand? Remember I am accustomed to winning the favors of kings, princes, cardinals. It is how we musicians earned our living. I charm them, they listen to me play, they see right away I am genius. The rest is simple. I will be very rich."

About three weeks into Gianni's overload phase, Nella Brandon came to me and said, "Dave, he's doing slice."

I don't know why I was surprised. I was.

"Are you sure?"

She nodded. "It's showing up in his blood, his urine, his metabolic charts. He probably does it every time he goes to play with that band. He's losing weight, corpuscle formation dropping off, resistance weakening. You've got to talk to him."

I went to him and said, "Gianni, I've stopped giving a damn what kind of music you write, but when it comes to drugs, I draw the line. You're still not completely sound physically. Remember, you were at the edge of death just a few months ago, body-time. I don't want you killing yourself."

"You do not own me." Again, sullenly.

"I have some claim on you. I want you to go on living."

"Slice will not kill me."

"It's killed plenty already."

"Not Pergolesi!" he snapped. Then he smiled, took my hand, gave me the full treatment. "Dave, Dave, you listen. I die once. I am not interested in an encore. But the slice, it is essential. Do you know? It divides one moment from the next. You have taken it? No? Then, you cannot understand. It puts spaces in time. It allows me to comprehend the most intricate rhythms, because with slice there is time for everything, the world slows down, the mind accelerates. Capisce? I need it for my music."

"You managed to write the Stabat Mater without slice."

"Different music. For this, I need it." He patted my hand. "You do not worry, eh? I look after myself."

What could I say? I grumbled, I muttered, I shrugged. I told Nella to keep a very close eye on his readouts. I told

Melissa to spend as much time as possible with him and keep him off the drug if she could manage it.

At the end of the month Gianni announced he would make his debut at The Quonch on the following Saturday. A big bill—five overload bands, Shining Orgasm Revival playing fourth, with Wilkes Booth John, no less, as the big group of the night. The kids in the audience would skull out completely if they knew that one of the Orgasms was three hundred years old, but of course they weren't going to find that out, so they'd just figure he was a new side-man and pay no attention. Later on Gianni would declare himself to be Pergolesi. He and Sam were already working on the altered PR program. I felt left out, off on another track. But it was beyond my control. Gianni now was like a force of nature, a hurricane of a man, frail and wan though he might be.

We all went to The Quonch for Gianni's overload debut.

There we sat, a dozen or more alleged adults, in that mob of screaming kids. Fumes, lights, colors, the buzzing of gadgetized clothes and jewels, people passing out, people coupling in the aisles, the whole crazy bit, like Babylon right before the end, and we sat through it. Kids selling slice, dole, coke, you name it, slipped among us. I wasn't buying but I think some of my people were. I closed my eyes and let it all wash over me, the rhythms and subliminals and ultrasonics of one group after another, Toad Star, then Bubblemilk, then Holy Ghosts, though I couldn't tell one from the next, and finally, after many hours, Shining Orgasm Revival was supposed to go on for its set.

A long intermission dragged on and on. And on.

The kids, zonked and crazed, didn't mind at first. But after maybe half an hour they began to boo and throw things and pound on the walls. I looked at Sam, Sam looked at me, Nella Brandon murmured little worried things.

Then Melissa appeared from somewhere, tugged at my arm and whispered, "Dr. Leavis, you'd better come backstage. Mr. Hoaglund. Dr. Brandon."

They say that if you fear the worst, you keep the worst at bay. As we made our way through the bowels of The Quonch to the performers' territory, I imagined Gianni sprawled backstage, wired with full gear, eyes rigid, tongue sticking out—dead of a slice overdose. And all our fabulous project ruined in a crazy moment. So we went backstage and there were the members of Shining Orgasm Revival running in circles, and a cluster of Quonch personnel conferring urgently, and kids in full war-paint peering in the back way and trying to get through the cordon. And there was Gianni, wired with full overload gear, sprawled on the floor, shirtless, skin shiny with sweat, mottled with dull purplish spots, eyes rigid, tongue sticking out. Nella Brandon pushed everyone away and dropped down beside him. One of the Orgasms said to no one in particular, "He was real nervous, man, he kept slicing off more and more, we couldn't stop him, you know—"

Nella looked up at me. Her face was bleak.

"OD?" I said.

She nodded. She had the snout of an ultrahypo against Gianni's limp arm and she was giving him some kind of shot to try to bring him around. But even in A.D. 2008, dead is dead is dead.

* * * *

It was Melissa who said afterward through tears, "It was his karma to die young, don't you see? If he couldn't die in 1736, he was going to die fast here. He had no choice."

And I thought of the biography that had said of him long ago, "His ill health was probably due to his notorious profligacy." And I heard Sam Hoaglund's voice in my mind saying, "Nobody steps out of character forever. The real Pergolesi will take control." Yes. Gianni had always been on a collision course with death, I saw now; by scooping him from his own era we had only delayed things a few months. Self-destructive is as self-destructive does, and a change of scenery doesn't alter the case.

If that is so—if, as Melissa says, karma governs all—should we bother to try again? Do we reach into yesterday's yesterday for some other young genius dead too soon, Poe or Rimbaud or Caravaggio or Keats, and give him the second chance we had hoped to give Gianni? And watch him recapitulate his destiny, going down a second time? Mozart, as Sam once suggested? Benvenuto Cellini? Our net is wide and deep. All of the past is ours. But if we bring back another, and he willfully and heedlessly sends himself down the same old karmic chute, what have we gained, what have we achieved, what have we done to ourselves and to him? I think of Gianni, looking to be rich and famous at last, lying purpled on that floor. Would Shelley drown again? Would Van Gogh cut off the other ear before our eyes?

Perhaps someone more mature would be safer, eh? El Greco, Cervantes, Shakespeare? But then we might behold Shakespeare signing up in Hollywood, El Greco operating out of some trendy gallery, Cervantes sitting down with his agent to figure tax-shelter angles. Yes? No. I look at the scoop. The scoop looks at me. It is very very late to consider these matters, my friends. Years of our lives consumed, billions of dollars spent, the seals of time ripped open, a young genius's strange odyssey ending on the floor backstage at The Quonch, and for what, for what, for what? We can't simply abandon the project now, can we?

Can we?

I look at the scoop. The scoop looks at me.

THE END

SCIENCE FICTION GRAND MASTERS SERIES

The Award Winning and Nominated Stories of

ROBERT SILVERBERG

DANGEROUS DIMENSIONS

Includes the Hugo Award Winning Story, *NIGHTWINGS*

AROUND THE CONTINUUM

Includes the Hugo Award Winning Story, *GILGAMESH IN THE OUTBACK*

BEYOND THE BEYOND

Including the Nebula Award Winning Story, *PASSENGERS*

ACROSS THE EONS

Includes the Nebula Award Winning Story, *SAILING TO BYZANTIUM*

WONDERS AND MARVELS

Includes the Hugo Award Winning Story, *ENTER A SOLDIER. LATER: ENTER ANOTHER*

GALACTIC TRAVELERS

Includes the Nebula Award Winning Story, *GOOD NEWS FROM THE VATICAN*

FUTURES UNLIMITED

Includes the Nebula Award Winning Story, *BORN WITH THE DEAD*

Published by Wonder Publishing Group

www.WonderPublishingGroup.com

www.WonderEbooks.com

WONDER PUBLISHING GROUP